"Frank Miniter has written a cyber-thriller that packs a political punch—an intrigue-filled tale that proves once again that fiction can warn us about the future."

—Rich Lowry, editor of *National Review*

"*Kill Big Brother* is a 21st-century action-adventure with a machine gun pace! Read the first 10 pages and you won't be able to put it down. This is a fast-paced modern thriller with very real electronic eavesdropping revelations that will keep you awake at night. Move over Orwell, Frank Miniter has just penned the modern day *1984*!"

—Scott McEwen, #1 *New York Times* Bestselling
Co-Author of *American Sniper* and the
Nationally Bestselling *Sniper Elite* series of novels

"We are told we need to give up privacy for security. We are told technology has killed privacy anyway. Many are now giving in to these false premises. Frank Minter's present-day Winston Smith, a new and bold hero, refuses to give in. In the throes of a thrilling ride he finds the very thing we've been searching for. Read *Kill Big Brother* and you'll know too."

—Keith Korman, author of
End Time, Eden: The Animals' Parable, and other novels

"It has always been a privilege for me to read Frank Miniter."

—Avik Roy, opinion editor for *Forbes*

"At a moment when government is expanding and individual liberties are up for debate, Frank Miniter has written a riveting defense of freedom."

—Pratik Chougule, executive editor of
The American Conservative

"*Kill Big Brother* is a brilliant account of ordeal by cyber terror. Open it and you won't want to put it down. When you do, you'll know how we can keep our freedom in this digital age."

–Stephen Hunter, bestselling author of the Bob Lee Swagger series of thrillers, and a Pulitzer Prize-winning film critic

KILL
BIG
BROTHER

FRANK MINITER

Post Hill
PRESS

A POST HILL PRESS BOOK
ISBN: 978-1-68261-469-3
ISBN (eBook): 978-1-68261-470-9

Kill Big Brother
© 2017 by Frank Miniter
All Rights Reserved

Cover Illustration by Brad Walker

Post Hill Press
New York • Nashville
posthillpress.com

Published in the United States of America

Dedication

To the often misunderstood, diminished, and even disregarded,
but still so beautiful U.S. Bill of Rights.

1

PREPARE TO BE CLEANSED

IF YOU SAW me on the morning when my whole life blew up so big it nearly took everyone else down with me you'd have thought . . . well, strike that, you wouldn't have thought anything. I designed this guy to be someone no normal person would look at twice. He is not even repulsive in an interesting sort of way. No, that would be too memorable. I was trying to stay alive and the best way for me to do that was to be a frumpy, pasty, middle-aged nobody in cheap, common clothes that were also bulletproof.

I am not speaking metaphorically here. The fat suit strapped around my middle was bulletproof body armor, which as any soldier who served in the Middle East can tell you, means it's heavy, itchy, and hot. But it wasn't hard, plated armor on the outside. On the surface this suit was made to actually feel like fat—soft, sweaty blubber. Now that sounds kind of interesting I guess in a disgusting sort of way. But try wearing it on a New York subway during the morning rush, as I did every morning and evening for a month, and you'll find this part loses its charm pretty fast.

Here's a snippet of how this particular undercover day began. There I was holding an overhead strap when the subway's cars jolted forward as they started out of the 59th Street station. Like everyone does every time, I fell off balance and my fake stomach squished into a woman's hand.

She winced like she'd touched a fat man's sweaty, white fish belly of hair-slathered fat rolls, gasped from shock, and pushed back into people behind her, sending a tremor passing through the crowded subway car at 8:00 a.m.

Now sure, I blushed behind my fake glasses and bit my lower lip as I looked down over my beige raincoat and at the worn brown wingtips on my feet, but what I was really thinking was this undercover part wasn't just dreary but also humiliating.

Okay, no one knew it was me behind the pasty skin, yellow teeth, bad hair extensions, and heavy glasses. But there is a point when any undercover part, just like any real part we play at a job, has the risk of actually becoming us and, as I said, I'd been playing this guy for a month already. I could feel myself, day by day, becoming this boob named Michael Waters.

So why did I purposely manufacture this part right down to his Social Security number and lame Facebook profile whose seven friends include a cat? Because no one would ever suspect this kind of a guy of being a modern private eye, a dude who has nabbed corporate moles pilfering millions and who has stopped international hacking syndicates financed by the Chinese government or by the Russians.

And when I was done with a job I needed to be able to disappear, so that, you know, I could go on living. I needed to be able to toss away the fake person as I seamlessly became someone else.

So there I was on this wet morning in October riding the subway to my current contract with no idea everything was about to come tumbling down. The train clanked to a stop beneath

Grand Central Station and the doors banged open and I stepped out with the mass of rushing commuters and walked fast, heel to toe, as my fake, bulletproof stomach shook just enough to make me waddle like a duck. All around the sound of everyone's clomping feet mingled with the clatter of the underground trains so loud it almost drowned out a saxophone someone was playing near the turnstiles.

I went up grimy tiled stairs into Grand Central Station's main room where Cary Grant once rushed through in *North by Northwest* thinking I was also an actor, only my life depended on not being seen as the leading man, the hero of any story. Now, I always like that the sound of hard-heeled shoes clunking on the station's stone floor echo off the high celestial ceiling making a sound like distant applause, but on this morning I was slouching under the weight of the body armor and desperately trying to see a way to catch this particular bad guy or gal so I could be myself again.

I stepped onto an escalator and went up to the north entrance of the station and advanced with other dark topcoats out revolving doors to sidewalks sheening silver from the autumn rain. I fumbled, as was my part, as I opened my black umbrella, and waddled beneath high-rises and by election posters on lampposts screaming about a presidential debate scheduled for Sunday night at The Garden.

I went through a high-rise's revolving glass doors while reminding myself to stay in character, that I was a computer troubleshooter named Michael Waters, a middle-aged, single nonentity who worked with computers because, as anyone could plainly see, he couldn't look people in the eyes. The security guard at an enormous marble security station glanced at my ID, then at me briefly before looking quickly away, and nodded me through. I put the ID away and stepped onto an elevator stuffed with wet coats and knew someone owned a dog. My stomach bumped into some poor guy—I still wasn't used to its foot-deep mass of body armor and gelatin. I stepped out at the twelfth floor and put my ID in front of a scanner at a glass door.

No beep. I tried again. No beep. A little blonde thing giggled at my ridiculousness and swiped her ID. I followed her in, troubled that my ID wouldn't work.

I wended through a maze of cubicles to a six-by-eight-foot cubbyhole allotted to Michael Waters. I stopped abruptly at the cubicle's entrance with a wet umbrella dripping in my hand, my face falling in shock, and my mouth open as I breathed—playing this part had become too natural.

My manager was in my chair. The skeletal little thirty-year-old man named Alexander had black-rimmed glasses, hair receding into his ears, and a black suit, always a freshly pressed black Stafford with a blue Van Heusen dress shirt. His eyes were in a perpetual and very judgmental squint, as if he was always pondering everyone else's pathetic part.

Alexander didn't rise when he saw my slouching, bulky body dripping with rain and perspiration, but just kept clicking away on the keyboard.

I didn't like this tepid, brittle little man. The receding hair, the horn-rims, the bloodless face only served to accentuate the man's role as the office backstabber.

Alexander finally looked up from my workstation and asked, "Are you Michael today? Or maybe Sidney? Or one of these other names?"

I stepped back. Almost ran away down the aisle of cubicles.

"In any event," Alexander said with the same arrogant tone, "security will walk you out."

My mouth went dry and my eyes were searching his face through my Coke-bottle lenses.

"I took the precaution of informing security," said the translucent bureaucrat, "but you can gather your personal items first."

A linebacker-sized security guard appeared at the edge of the aisle of cubicles and lumbered gravely toward us. Eyes peeped over the tops of cubicle walls like so many prairie dogs.

None of the pencils or pictures were mine, mine really. The junk was all just part of this idiotic false identity. I didn't need them. Didn't want them. No point in giving Alexander or the beefy guy from security the satisfaction anyway.

I did want to know why however. "Alexander, how did . . . ?"

Alexander smiled without showing any teeth before he answered. "It came from the top first thing. They said you are not who you say you are. That you're up to no good. Leave your laptop and your BlackBerry on the desk. They're our property. No charges are being filed now, whatever your real name is. After I search your hard drive that'll change. I've seen what you've been up to on the server. You've been everywhere. Somehow you got passwords. When I find out what you've done, they'll be charges, I'm sure of that."

I dropped Waters' computer bag and corporate BlackBerry on the desk and wanted to say, "Of course I've been all over the system. I was hired by upper management to find a corporate thief." But I didn't. Instead I handed over my ID and watched this insipid, weak, little man attempt to cut it in half, only to struggle to push scissors through thick plastic.

I should have been at least slightly amused by this, but was way too befuddled to enjoy the moment.

I turned and lumbered away silently with the security guard following, swaggering. I could feel people watching from their endless boxes. Eyes tracking me, voices whispering, "Who is that guy anyway? Didn't he just start?"

Nobody likes playing a guilty person.

2

EVERYONE KNOWS EVERYTHING

THE ELEVATOR DOORS shut and the security guard said, "Sorry, buddy."

There was a large, gray nameplate pinned to the guard's shirt that actually read "Winston Smith." I ran my eyes up the guard's chest to a head that had to stoop through doorways and saw the expression of a sympathetic drone. The nametag was likely some inside joke from a George Orwell fan so I didn't ask, didn't say how damn appropriate it really was.

The elevator stopped, the doors slid open. We walked into a lobby under gaudy chandeliers. The guards at the security desk outside the elevator bank stared as we walked by. All the people in the business suits walking to the elevators seemed to grasp intuitively what was happening. Someone was being cut from the herd. A person was being shunned. They'd gossip about this for a few minutes and then forget all about it. No one recognized this pudgy loser of a man named Waters anyway.

With the guard a step behind I went out revolving doors onto the sidewalk and found myself wishing the swaggering leviathan would toss me violently into passersby along the wet walkway; at least that would be an acknowledgment I was somebody, even if a no-good somebody. Left this way I only felt like a garbage bag being indifferently tossed into a Dumpster.

The guard threatened because he thought he was supposed to: "Don't come back. We'll be watching." Then the big man with the fitting nametag turned and lumbered back into the high-rise.

I walked slowly away with my shoulders slouching under the weight of the body armor. Rain trickled down my neck, beaded on my glasses. New Yorkers' umbrellas collided with each other sending droplets showering over me. I didn't notice. Didn't even pull out my umbrella. I'd always thought if I was found out it would be by someone very much interested in either getting away or killing me. Those were real reactions. This was just embarrassing.

An iPhone I'd purchased with another identity vibrated from beneath my raincoat. I fumbled for it and pulled it from my suit jacket's breast pocket. I looked at the phone as I robotically waddled to nowhere in particular. A text message read: "We know all the parts you play. You are being cleansed of all your falsity."

I stopped. Like a logjam in a stream, I stood steadfast as a current of people beat against me, parting around me in the crisp October air. Rain droplets formed on the iPhone's screen. I watched the tiny drops slip, slide down.

Minutes ticked by in this semiconscious state until I finally put the phone away, only to feel it vibrate again.

I put the phone to my ear and heard a recorded voice say, "Sidney, it's your father."

I stepped out of the way of people with things to do and leaned against a brick building. My father's voice made me shudder, made me wish I hadn't voice-identified all of my usual callers. I took the call.

"Son! This is my only phone call."

In jail?

"What happened?"

"They say I stole money. They say I was brokering again."

"But you lost your license years ago."

"I know. I know. It's crazy, but they have all this evidence that I was doing a Ponzi. They say someone emailed it to them."

The voice sounded soberer than in years.

"Who are *they*, Dad?"

"I don't know. Some anonymous . . . son, I need a lawyer. They say I won't make bail. I don't know."

The voice was shaky. My father needed a drink.

After taking directions to the proper precinct, I said, "I'll do what I can."

I walked slowly south along Park Avenue, going in the direction of my Manhattan apartment, my Fortress of Solitude, to the apartment I kept when I was between contracts, when I just wanted to fade away and recharge. I kept stopping to watch for tails. I was too numb to really watch.

I stopped in a corner coffee shop and bought a latte. I sat on a stool where I could see out a window, but couldn't be easily spotted. As I sipped the latte I watched people under umbrellas passing by. It was always so damn hard to spot a tail in New York, as everyone seems to fit in Manhattan. A person would have to paint their body blue and howl like a wolf to stand out on these streets. Though even then, New Yorkers would just shrug, police would laugh, and somebody would stick it on Facebook. On the Upper East Side they might not even bother.

I rested my head on my right hand and inspected each passerby. As a computer forensics investigator, I often have to profile people as I hunt for a corporate thief. I've learned to control myself and think clearly when others panic. I tried to still my mind as I watched the people striding by.

I took off my fake glasses and rubbed my eyes. I looked down at the fake stomach and wondered: Am I a clown? Should I just take off these costumes? Is that what being cleansed means? What is going on? Who is after me?

I didn't know.

After thirty minutes I left the coffee shop and took subways south, north, then south again.

I walked up the cement stairs out of a subway and turned a corner. I waited and watched again before using an ID to electronically open a glass door into the apartment building.

The elevator took me to the tenth floor and I got off. The building was pre-World War II but had been refurbished and so was clean and quiet. I stopped in the hall and logged on to my home-security system with my iPhone. The apartment's alarm hadn't been tripped and the motion sensors inside hadn't been triggered. I sighed and took out a key, unlocked the metal door, and entered my haven breathing relief in a city so big I could be anonymous, almost.

I shut the door and locked it and leaned against it. I rubbed my temples and breathed long, deep mouthfuls of stale apartment air.

I walked over a hardwood floor and took off my glasses. I pulled off the raincoat and a cheap gray suit and then the fat suit and tossed them in a corner. I put my head in a sink and washed out as much of the gray as I could and pulled out the hair extensions. I used a teeth-whitening kit to bleach away Michael Waters' yellow teeth. I pulled off the rest of the idiotic costume and looked at myself in the bathroom mirror for a long minute. I felt like a clown who'd pulled off his rubber nose for the last time while wondering, *who am I now?*

I walked into the apartment's main room and stared at my laptop computer and took a deep breath before logging on. There were hundreds of emails in my accounts. Many were from people I didn't know anymore. All were saying they never really knew me. But now they did. Oh, how they did. Someone had sent them my personal thoughts. What I'd said online, over the phone, even stuff from my hard drives. They knew which websites I'd logged on to and the porn I'd viewed and the books I'd bought, taken from the library. Everything was all out into the world. My grades, medical records, criminal record . . . all public. Oh, nothing too horrible in the records. Just dumb little things, like the time I was caught with an open container. Like the time I emailed a friend I was dumping so-and-so because she was "narcissistic." Stupid things. Personal things. And all the undercover parts I'd played and people I'd busted were there too. There were photos and videos. There were links to records of the people who went to jail.

Hours passed. I got text messages, emails, phone calls from old flames: "If I only knew you before. How you really felt. Who you really were."

From old friends: "Sidney, did you really stop talking to me because I was cheating on Catherine?"

From a few corporate contacts: "I hired you because I wanted our loss of records kept quiet. Now it's public that our tech was stolen. Our stock is tumbling. A video of me hiring you is on the Web. You can expect to hear from our attorneys."

From people I'd taken down: "I know who and where you are now!"

I called the precinct that held my father. "Bail hasn't been set yet, but it's gonna be high," cuffed a desk sergeant.

I hung up the phone.

I dropped my head into my hands.

3

THE RELUCTANT AGENT

HOURS PASSED BEFORE I pulled my mind out of the cyberworld long enough to peer out my apartment's tenth-floor window. The rain had blown away, leaving a dark blue sky. October sun was overexposing glass high-rises.

Emails were still flooding in from friends, from people forgotten, from the press, from U.S. Securities and Exchange Commission investigators. My phone had silently buzzed dozens of times. The jobs I'd been contracted to do were cancelled. An executive whispered into the phone that their business deal had been made public, that my contract had been emailed company wide, that reporters were calling, that they might seek legal action.

I leaned back violently into my chair and put my hands over my face. Killing me would have been less painless and so much simpler. The Chinese were sophisticated enough to manage this, but why would they? The Russians . . . forget about it. Who else? One of the hackers I'd sent to jail?

I took my hands away from my face and saw emails popping into my various email accounts from banks, such as UBS, one of the Swiss banks I used, and from NCB Cayman Limited, and from other banks and I began to shout profanity and to stomp around like an upset child.

Profanity helped, a little.

I got control of myself and saw that all my banks were saying my accounts had been frozen, that the IRS was investigating, that some funds, the ones the IRS could get to, had been seized already. Sure, international and federal banking laws gave them this power, depending on the nation involved, but I never saw this orchestrated attack coming. How did they find all my accounts? They weren't even in my name. They were just numbered bank accounts. And I'd paid my taxes, though I didn't know how the hell I'd prove that. I'd been paid from corporate slush funds via international money wires. The corporations wanted it this way so they could hide the fact they were rooting out corporate espionage, that their secret wonder drugs had been swiped by foreign pharmaceutical companies, or that their financial reports were being hacked and sold to investors before they were publicly released.

I'd lost everything. My name, reputation, privacy, money . . . were all gone. Next might be my freedom, maybe my life.

Other calls, texts, and emails were from employees I'd made friends with as I'd worked undercover. Two were threats. People I'd helped bust. They said they knew where I lived, had my real photo. Most of the calls were from low-level peons, people who didn't even know what I'd been doing for their companies, people who were calling to say they were no longer in need of my services. Reasons varied, but their fear didn't; it was intense and fatal, like they were talking to a victim of the plague.

Then the IRS called. They actually called. I just hung up on the jerk and left my apartment. The afternoon was warm. I needed to walk to clear my mind. The IRS wanted a full audit. They wanted full disclosure and somehow they'd already gotten it. I'd been honest, at least as much as I could be. I was working in a field regulation had yet to catch. How would they understand that the people who hired me did so because I wasn't only good but also completely confidential? Why would they believe I'd been honest? Facts would get twisted. Partial truths from forked-tongue lawyers would destroy me. I was at the mercy of IRS bureaucrats. I was guilty until proven innocent. I recalled that the English poet William Blake once quipped he was "innocent until proven broke."

I strode along Manhattan's living streets as the afternoon sun flared orange, giving the city a soft, Technicolor hue. Rain had washed the detritus from millions of passersby away. The sidewalks and lampposts were a dark wet, adding contrast to the warm, orange light. Florid autumn air blew from the forests somewhere west. People inhaled the fresh fall air, summer humidity all gone, and felt easier, even let their Manhattan strides slow, a little.

It didn't give me any peace. Like I just stepped off a plane, my ears felt like they were clogged just short of popping. I heard taxi horns as a hum, conversations as mumbles, bus engines as low grumbles.

One, two, three hours passed like a head rush. My phone continued to vibrate. I turned it off. It kept ringing in my head.

I finally wandered back in the late afternoon. I didn't know who might be responsible. There were many who would like to do this to me, yet I couldn't think of anyone who could pull it off. Not knowing who was the most disturbing part.

I was so lost in this dilemma I didn't see the dark suit step in front. Another behind. I walked right into the goon as hands grabbed my arms and a paper bag was pulled over my head. I struggled. I felt like a child wrestling with football stars. My wrists were handcuffed behind my back. Hands searched my pockets. Someone took my phone. I heard someone take its battery out. Men picked me up by my arms. Big men carried me across a sidewalk, between parked cars. A mitt-sized hand muzzled me.

I kicked spasmodically, like a person at the end of a rope. I was dropped as casually as groceries into a Town Car's back seat. Someone sat stiffly against the far door, another sat beside me. I found myself in the middle. The car entered traffic.

I stopped struggling and demanded from the paper bag, "What do you want? Who are you?"

Someone chuckled.

Shoulders hard with muscle pressed from both sides. It was like being packed in a subway car at rush hour with the entire Bulgarian Olympic wrestling team. All I could see was brown paper. All I could smell was cheese, Limburger.

The one in the front passenger seat spoke: "Relax, Sidney. You're in no danger."

"I don't know about that!" said the driver.

Their accents were Mid-Atlantic. They weren't Bronx muscle, or international mercenaries. They were square, solid. I relaxed. I knew my parts well and these were government employees—FBI or some other federal acronym. These were the muscle. I was going to meet the brains. I'd save my energy for the know-it-all.

My face grew hot from my breath. The paper bag rustled every time I exhaled. The smell of cheese was giving me nausea. This was probably the bag they'd gotten their lunch in from some Manhattan deli. Yeah, I could even see grease stains from some hot pastrami or Reuben. What a bunch of bozos. Maybe the bag over my head was an afterthought.

The car stopped. They hadn't left Midtown. Couldn't have. They'd only turned five times—two lefts, a right, then a left and a right. At that speed they couldn't have gone more than twenty blocks. I didn't hear any tunnels or bridges. They couldn't have made it downtown to the FBI's offices at 26 Federal Plaza.

"We can't be downtown at G-man HQ already," I said.

"A savvy geek, huh!" said one.

I was hoisted again and carried paper-bag-still-on-my-head up ten stairs and through squeaky doors, then down a hall and onto an old elevator. I stood in a tiny elevator pressed on all sides by big men who lifted weights for recreation. We went up two floors. I was pushed out elevator doors and shoved across a hall and through another door. A large wood door slammed behind. One of them yanked the cheesy bag off my head.

I blinked and saw an apartment with high ceilings, expensive moldings, and thick, blue curtains drawn over windows. This must be a brownstone somewhere in Midtown. People were moving all around. The place was dank, but busy.

One person wasn't moving. This fifty-something, bald, fat man, in a double-breasted gray suit as worn as grandpa's flannel pajamas had a cigar stuck in a frown and was leaning on a fireplace mantle staring at me.

"Have a seat, Sidney," said the fat man as he pointed to a wooden desk chair.

I sat down. Crossed my legs. Waited. Questions cascaded through my mind. Anger at first drowned out observations, then fury left and I regained composure. Without moving my head I saw technicians preparing electronics. I felt calmer as I understood what they were doing. I was to be questioned. They wanted something from me. As long as they needed something from me, whatever it was, I had some margin of control. Having a hand to play improved my disposition.

A minute ticked past before the fat man said, "You're a quiet, controlled one aren't you?"

"You're feds," I said, relieved that my voice was calmer than my mind. "I'm hoping you have answers. I'm waiting to hear them."

"Answers? To what?"

I shot my eyes around the room, then back to the fat man and said, "First, take off these cuffs."

The fat man pointed his cigar at someone behind and keys jingled and the cuffs were taken off.

I exhaled and rubbed my wrists. I tried to deaden my expression. This cop had interrogated before; he wanted to see my hand before committing. He wanted me to let my barriers down first. He wanted to maintain control. This was a power play.

I looked up then down this fat man and decided not to give the bureaucrat the satisfaction.

Another minute passed before the government man pulled his arm off the mantle and turned to face me square shouldered. This was a pose the fat FBI man had chosen to maintain authority. But with me quietly staring back he began to feel fatter than usual, more self-conscious than normal.

"Why are you staring at me like that?"

I was weary of looking at this obese man in the rumpled suit, so I shrugged, asked, "Okay, why am I here?"

"Ah, inquisitive at last! That's better. Now, sit still."

Three men with white shirtsleeves rolled up surrounded me. They unbuttoned my shirt, attached a lie detector to my hands and chest. They put a silver, kooky-looking cap, with wires feeding into a computer, on my head. They taped heat sensors to my forehead, wrists, and heart. They put on meters that would read my heartbeat, pulse, and blood pressure. They placed a camera in front of my face. Someone took my picture. Another person scanned my eyes with a biometric reader. Someone told me to answer all questions into the video camera's unblinking glass eye.

"If you move we'll have to strap you down."

This was annoying. I knew what all this was. They were going to read my thoughts, based on my facial movements, eye dilations, brain waves, heart rate, shifts in the tone of my voice. Once the technicians achieved a baseline they'd know if I was lying, but they could do so much more. The dilation of my eyes, the flaring of my nostrils, the slight changes in skin tone, in my skin's heat, and more would tell them about my fear, anxiety, hope, evasiveness. The neuroimaging cap on my head would read my brain waves and compare the firing of the synapses in regions of my brain to thousands of others who'd undergone this treatment. The cap was linked to a functional transcranial Doppler that would read my thoughts by monitoring my brain's activity. This software would attempt to read my thoughts with cognitive polygraph software, brain fingerprinting analysis, and other programs running simultaneously to profile and see through me. Though this science was still young, neuroscientists at Carnegie Mellon University proved they could read letters and some basic thoughts from this type of brain imagery. I didn't know how much further the NSA had gotten with this technology.

"You're NSA," I said.

"Some are," grumbled the fat man while chewing his cigar.

"You want to read me, to see right into me. I know what all this software is. But these digital eyes aren't the truth serum you hope they are."

"Maybe not," said the fat man, "but you might be surprised."

"All they'll give you are averages. Which means you'll always be wrong at the important times."

The fat man chuckled and sat down in a comfortable-looking leather lounge a dozen feet in front of me before saying, "We have a lot of ways to get the truth from you. This one is just the most legal and it's pain-free. There are other things we can do with you. We know you've broken a lot of laws. You've hacked a lot of government systems and have fake IDs right here in your wallet. These are felonies."

The fat man smiled boorishly.

I don't like threats. I detested how authoritarian this government goon was behaving. I felt as if I were suddenly a twelve-year-old again sitting on the little metal chair in front of

Miss Vanobitch's big oak desk; my old middle school principal, the witch with the gap in her front teeth that shot spit when she seethed; the gray woman who'd glibly told me college was no place for me, that I belonged in a ditch. A horrible proclamation spoken just weeks after my mother had died and my father had begun to drink. Mean words coughed up by an authority figure after I'd fought a bully on the playground and won. Something I'd wanted to do forever, but never dared, not until I was pushed into an emotional wall, not until I no longer cared. She'd judged me and pointed to the path I must walk like she was some ancient Greek soothsayer, yet she didn't even know me. Now I was looking at another smug authority figure, someone who thought he controlled me as Vanobitch had. But that style of bullying didn't even work in my insecure youth.

"We don't have to get a judge to deny bail, do we?"

My eyes narrowed. Little wrinkles creased at their edges. Behind me a computer technician smiled. I was reacting. My truth was coming out. They were getting a rise out of me. They were getting what they wanted.

I stared into the black hole at the center of the fat man's brown irises while considering how much harm this government man could do to me. After concluding not much, I asked, "What's the address here? I think I'll have my attorney over to join us."

"Sure," said the fat man without hesitation, "but we can't help you then."

"Help? Is that what you call your secret police carrying me off for electronic interrogation?"

"This isn't like that."

"Isn't it though? You haven't even introduced yourself. I don't like hardball. You want my help with something, play me straight. All you're doing now is making me get stubborn."

I moved my gaze to an NSA technician on my right and asked, "Am I lying?"

"All right," interrupted the fat man as the technician smirked, "you can have your attorney. This is a *free country.*"

A moment of silence passed as the fat man bit on his cigar, then he said, "Before you make that damn mistake let me tell you how it is."

The fat man leaned back into his hard leather chair and took a long pull, making his cigar's tip flare fluorescent, before he asked, "Have you met yourself yet?"

"Huh?"

"Yourself?"

"I don't get it."

"Good. That's to come. We got you quick. There's a chance."

I opened my mouth sarcastically and lifted my left eyebrow. A technician sighed behind me.

The fat man smiled, exposed round, yellow teeth, an expression that said he liked that I had a strong ego. "My name's Bill Rooney. Everyone calls me Rooney. I'm a special agent with the Federal Bureau of Investigation. We know you're being cleansed. We know who is doing it, well . . . we don't know who the Truth Seekers are, but that's what you're going to help us with, isn't it?"

I dramatically nodded, twitched my nose, puckered and un-puckered my lips. I knew the technicians were getting their baseline, so I exaggerated all my emotions to throw them off, to toy with them. I needed to hide something. To have something left, held secret. I was being publicly raped of everything. I'd have to start a new identity, to start completely over. But all that was to come. First I needed answers. I needed to know who was behind this, because they could do it again, anytime.

"I see you're ascertaining, adjusting, good. I'll give you a little help," Rooney said as his fat cheeks shook. "The Truth Seekers are an online cult led by a man who calls himself Verity."

"Verity?" I said. I'd heard of him or her. "But doesn't this Verity just go after politicians? I haven't seen anything about that profiler going after private citizens. If, that is, this Verity nut really exists."

"Oh, he exists," said Rooney. "In fact, we have reason to believe he and his Truth Seekers have infiltrated Google, Yahoo, Acxiom, ChoicePoint, Verifications Inc., and more. Our cyberwarriors are hunting them with a few successes. But these Truth Seekers are all separate tentacles attached to a head. We have to get the brains, to get Verity, as no Truth Seeker knows more than one other Truth Seeker and none of them seems to know who Verity is.

"And now Verity has decided to recruit you," Rooney said, pointing his cigar at me. "He goes after talent. The Truth Seekers start by exposing people to themselves. They reveal everything. If the victim handles it, can look themselves in the eye, is pure, honest enough to deal with the world knowing everything about them, then they tow them in. They convert them to their ideology. They use them to . . . oh, we'll get to all that later. First, we need you on board. We'll get the IRS off you and expunge anything you've ever done; we'll even, after all of this, help you get your identity back. We'll do what we can for your father. But first you have to agree to become an informant, to go along with Verity, to join him, and then to help us get him. And you'll have to learn to follow the rules."

I was still perplexed. "That profiler who's all over the news? I don't get it?" I said while miming an expression used to frighten small children.

I'd been following the Verity story. The only part of the upcoming election that intrigued me was this so-called Verity character, a captivating villain who'd been dredging up dirt on politicians by hacking private computers, eavesdropping on communications, and sending the saucy stuff to reporters all the while hiding behind the anonymity of an internet pseudonym. I knew the truth-telling rascal was being aggressively hunted by cyberwarriors at the NSA; in fact, the NSA geeks were being so aggressive they'd already scooped up dozens of murky characters in their dragnet—people who write computer viruses for no other reason than the nasty things pose a David-and-Goliath challenge to the establishment. All the hacker chats were gabbing about the incessant and invasive manhunt, so I, being a cyber private eye, could hardly miss the details of this side story, even while I was all wrapped up in my own hunt.

What made Verity all the more intriguing was that the reporters didn't like him, as his facts had an annoying habit of being second-sourced and right from the source. Worse, his info wasn't tweaked or spun with personal opinion. This profiler only gave the facts and nothing but the facts. The dirt wasn't even favorable to any particular party. As a result, most journalists just reported the provided information, after spinning it in their preferred political direction, of course. When they had to source the info, they typically said the source was anonymous. They seemed to like that word very much, as it made them seem like they had some Deep Throat informant, someone who was delivering info on top-secret government scandals right into their talented little hands, which made them seem so very important indeed.

Besides, the word from the federal agencies was that this Verity guy wasn't just one nut-ball anyway, but was a lot of disgruntled types dropping scandalous bombs on the party they didn't happen to root for. Most of the reporters seemed to agree with this analysis. After all, not even the NSA had been able to close in on this Verity. And Verity's dirt came from so many different IP addresses from all over the planet that he or she couldn't possibly be just one person. Every remailer in the world couldn't pull that act off, so the accepted narrative postulated by the federal agencies was that a lot of people were just anonymously acting as whistle-blowers while using this Verity name as cover.

There had been a lot of copycats cuffed already. You might even say it'd become a trend, a truth-telling epidemic even—in an election season no less. And whether it was the correct narrative or not, all that broken news was really ticking off the journalists, as their field was crowded enough already with all the bloggers these days—so much so that they were beginning to feel unappreciated. So they were reluctant to give this nom de plume dubbed Verity any respect whatsoever.

With all that in mind, I couldn't accept this conclusion. "But this Verity guy is just fiction. The FBI even says so."

"That's our official position, yes. But no, he's quite real I'm afraid; in fact, Verity will contact you soon," said Rooney as he watched me closely.

After a pause, Rooney began again with a more subdued tone. "He'll ask you to make a choice: to use his truth or not. You'll choose his path. You can't mention anything about us online, on the phone, or anywhere. There are no safe phones. By now he has your voice. Voice-recognition software will trigger a trace, at least we think that's how he does it. Anyway, he'll know. He always knows."

"That's not possible."

Rooney puffed his cheeks, blew smoke up at the ceiling, looked back at me and said, "Why not? We're getting better at it. Ever heard of Echelon, Carnivore, Total Information Awareness, EINSTEIN 2 or 3? So much damn stuff has gone public. But he's got some other . . . look, don't contact us. We'll contact you. We'll always be around, somewhere. Special Agent Bent here will lead the team detailed to you. It's too soon now to tell you more. Just go about your business and go along with Verity. Be hesitant. Be honest in your emotions. If he senses a lie, he'll walk away and leave you with the mess he's orchestrated. Do this and later we'll bring you in, give you the tools to help us. We'll be watching and in contact."

"What about the IRS, my father, the—"

"Not now. If we help you now, Verity will know, he always knows," Rooney said. "Just, no matter what happens, know we have your back."

I regained my composure and asked with a smile too constant even for a politician, "What does Verity want?"

Rooney shrugged and said as much to himself as to me, "To kill Big Brother."

"He's a conspiracy nut?"

Rooney's big, puffy eyes hardened as he said, "They'll be a time to explain those things. Will you work with us?"

It took everything in me to stop myself from throwing my chair at him. To him it was an easy thing to ask. To me, he was asking for all I had left, for my whole identity, to compromise everything I've worked for. I stalled. "Give me something in writing. An official intent that you'll do all the things you say and anything else I can think of."

"Can't do it. This is all top secret."

"You just expect me to trust you?"

Rooney smiled, exposing round, tobacco-stained teeth as he said, "What fucking choice do you have? You're naked!"

"Yeah, what choice do I have?" I said with exaggerated disdain the technician took for honest exasperation.

4

IS THIS FACE YOURS?

THE FBI AGENTS put another brown paper bag over my head—this one reeking of salami—and pushed me out of the apartment, down an elevator, and out an alley to a waiting Town Car. The car motored out of an alley and merged with traffic. After a left turn, two blocks, a right, and a dozen or so blocks north the bag came off.

Agent Bent was frowning in the rearview mirror as he handed something over the seat. "Here's your phone. And here's a personal locator beacon."

"A what?"

"A PLB. Trust me. We'd use smoke signals to avoid electronic surveillance if we could. Just hit the button on top if Verity contacts you. Its signal is at a frequency no one picks up but our satellites. Hit it anywhere satellites can pick up its signal and we'll know within three square feet of where you are. But when you do, don't look for us. We'll let you see us if we want you to see us."

The Town Car stopped at 5th and 42nd.

Agent Bent said, "Good luck meeting yourself."

I wanted to ask what the hell Bent was talking about, but I was pushed out onto the sidewalk. The door slammed. The car's tires squealed as it jumped into moving traffic.

I got to my feet and dusted sidewalk grime from my elbows. I walked west along 42nd Street while trying to absorb this new information. I kept wandering blindly with the multitudes of put-on faces and began thinking I'd long been a lone wolf, an only child, a motherless nonconformist, a solo computer forensics expert, a man who literally plays many parts. But I was never this alone, this much of a tool, a drone. My whole life was so suddenly wide open and the government had become my master. By safeguarding technology, by policing America's Fortune 500s, by nailing international corporate spies, I'd done more good for this country than people would ever know. I didn't need credit, but, I seethed, "No one owns me."

My legs tired and I sat on a sidewalk under the Empire State Building without realizing sitting on dirty cement wasn't something I'd normally do. The setting autumn sun tinted the glass along the concrete canyon's auburn. I looked up the stately high-rise to the sky, then back at the people pushing past on both sides of the street. The streetlights had come on, though it was still mostly light. I looked over all the people in their daily struggle from work to home. I wondered about my own part. For the first time I didn't feel in charge of my own actions.

I'd always been confident. Even when a boy I always knew what I wanted. After just two semesters at MIT I'd walked away, because I knew I should. By then I was already spending every hour coding, helping others safeguard their computer systems, tracking people online. My professors had a lot to teach, but not about what I was interested in. I was ahead of them with programming, with hacking, with understanding the Wild West that was the net in those days. Since then my career had come easy. I'd moved back to New York, my hometown, without my ex-stockbroker for a father even knowing. I picked up a contract helping an investment capital firm fend off Chinese hackers the next week. My success led to other contracts. My reputation preceded me. I kept learning, writing software, coding, hunting Wall Street's criminals online. I learned to create aliases. I learned to be anonymous, to stay clean, to be a ghost. But now this?

I looked up along the Empire State Building's long lines to the sky and said, "What can I do?"

I dropped my head into my hands. I hadn't felt so cynical, so hopeless since the months after my mother died when I was twelve. I felt like I was falling, yet there was no bottom. The unknown had me. I was being led, controlled by people, yet I didn't even know which way they'd make me run next. I felt like a character in a video game, a hero played by an amateur.

Then, out of the corner of an eye, was a flash of a face, a familiar face. I saw it for a brief moment and only in the peripheral. There and then gone. Not possible. Just seeing things in the dusk. It couldn't be. I looked again. Concentrated.

I stood and walked through a crowd pushing to subways.

There, I saw him again. The back of a head walking away. Hair a familiar color. A body shape I had long since stopped looking at, but knew intricately. Particulars in everyday things fade, but the brain still catches them, knows them. This person was familiar.

I quickened my pace, bumped into a small straw-haired thing Didn't stop. Too many people. There across the street. Running then. Taxi in the way. Stopped. Tossing my head.

Where is he? He was right here.

I leaned against a lamppost. It couldn't have been. I shook my head. I rubbed my temples. Closed my eyes. Breathed deeply. Began rubbing circles, circles, soothing circles on my temples. It seemed to help. Pressure alleviated. The horns and voices, autos and people, faded away to a light hum. Breathing, rubbing circles, feeling the cold metal of a lamppost, I pretended it was a boulder up on the Shawangunk, a mountain ridge I sometimes go to for solace. The air was cool. All around became peace. Anxiety faded. I stopped rubbing circles on my temples, opened my eyes, and looked up.

And saw myself staring back with a look of equal astonishment.

Across the street, leaning against a lamppost, stood my double. Standing in the same pose, dressed in the same clothes, wearing the same weary face, was my twin—the identical type. I stood straight with surprise. My double did the same. I took a step back. My double did the same. I attempted to cross the street, but was cut off by a taxi. My double did the same, acting like a taxi crossed his path. The street cleared thanks to a red light and I bolted across at my double, who turned and ran, mimicking my toe-to-heel sprint perfectly. We matched stride for stride up a side street like equally matched runners in a marathon.

Tiring, five blocks into the run, I couldn't gain a step, but began to find that when I slowed, my double did the same. I reduced my sprint to a jog, then to a walk. Treading thirty feet apart we went from block to block as I formed a plan. As I caught my breath, I began to think that I just needed to wait for something to hinder my double's progress, anything that would give me an advantage. Then my look-alike turned right into an alley.

I stopped, stalled. I was uncertain and that damn gut of mine, my barometer, wasn't giving me any advice. It could be a trap. Should I follow myself into a dark alley? The question was preposterous. Curiosity, the need to know, overwhelmed me and I turned into the alley. I peeked in. In the back, alone, my double was bent forward, miming my movements. Rage overcame my hesitance. I swaggered in, furious. My twin, with the same irate eyes, set jaw, ripe sweater, and dark slacks, swaggered forward. We stopped, each eyeing the other up and down.

I saw my anger turn to trepidation on a mirror image. Then to anger again as I realized I was being mocked. I took another step forward with the intention of flogging the rogue, but again stopped. I would feel strange fighting myself. This uncertainty kept me thinking: *Should I grab him and force him to talk? Can I?*

I gained some confidence from the fact that this impersonator was cornered. So I shouted, as if the boom of my voice would add to my certitude, "Who are you?"

"Who are you?" answered the impostor in the same voice, but with a slight tone shift. I would have sworn it was my own voice, but I wasn't being mimicked like a school child; I was being asked the question.

On the defensive then, I said, "I'm Sidney McDaniel."

"Funny, that's my name."

Voice gruff, gaining volume, "You're . . . you're impersonating me."

"Oh, do you own this face? Do you have this nose trademarked? These eyes registered?"

"Well, no, but—"

"You don't have a legitimate claim to these looks, do you? Someone can wear them so easily. To a degree, looks and image, after all, can be changed like clothes. The surface is a canvas that can be painted with many colors. You of all people should know that. You play so many parts."

"Who are you?"

"Why I'm you today. Can't you tell?"

"How did you find me?"

"I've always been with you. Is a reflection never given a day to speak?"

I shook my head, demanded, "What do you want?"

"You to understand who you are. Look at this face. Hear this voice. You've used them you know. They've given you advantages. We're likable. We're dominant. We're good looking!"

"But, but . . . it's what's inside that matters."

"That old cliché. Yes of course, but first you must acknowledge what's on the outside. You must take your looks into consideration, you must control them, understand them, or they'll control you. Because they're not you . . . unless you let them be."

I looked at my face worn by another and wondered if I always looked that sure, that calm, that accepting. I never thought my voice was so flat and penetrating. I wasn't sure I liked the way I looked at people, like I was waiting through a commercial. I decided my frosted hair was a bit immature and my posture a bit too straight. I wondered if I really walked like I had a shield around me. I began to understand why I had so few friends my age.

My double said, "You're starting to see, aren't you? It's all here in your face, posture, and pose. Look deeply. Looks must be taken into account; they must be understood so they can be put aside. You're lucky. Yours are good, if common. They fit into this society. You're accepted."

I saw that much.

"And by now you know you're guilty," said my double. "You accepted income off the books and then broke the IRS's rules to declare it. You created false identities by filing false documents. You lied, you deceived. You're warped. Can you handle your falsification? Can you handle yourself? At least your alcoholic father knows who he is! All those girls you dated, but never let in. Now you see why it never worked. You're arrogant and think you're open, judgmental and think you're accepting. You play other people, but you have no idea who you are. You have a lot to learn."

My eyes searched his as my voice faltered but managed, "How dare you. What is this?"

"Your cleansing."

"What . . . I . . . ?"

"Only the knowledge of who you are can set you free. You're guilty, corrupted. You must pay for your sins before . . . you'll see."

This confusing, judgmental statement angered me. Though I hadn't been in a fight since grade school, in a fury, an impulse, I lurched forward, grabbed my double, and we started to spin round and round until he tossed me off-balance to the ground.

I leapt back up and attempted to tackle. My twin spun me and on we went pushing and shoving down the alley. Grunting. Gasping. Tiring. I tried to swing my double off balance, but he swung his hips and threw me into a brick wall.

I jumped up. Charged. Missed. Rose again. Charged, head down. We grappled, started to spin. Though our sweaters seemed to hide the same girth, he had spent more time in a gym. This actor was stronger, faster, he threw me to the ground by turning his hips again and letting my weight move by him.

Dirt smeared with blood on my cheek. My double contemptuously dusted his knees. Something had changed. The man was no longer acting. He was showing his true posture and role. Somehow, he didn't even look like me anymore. I watched him walk behind a Dumpster, pull out a blue binder six inches thick, and throw it at my feet.

"Read it. It's your profile. It's already been released to many you know. The IRS needn't audit. Your friends and colleagues needn't investigate. It's all there. Time to face yourself."

The voice was no longer his, but was contemptuous of me.

The condescension flooded strength into me. I pounced. I tackled low, smashing with my shoulders into my double's knees. Then I was on top, holding my persecutor's face in the dirt with the power of burning rage. I saw this look-alike was wearing a mask. I started to pull it off as I demanded, "Who, who are you?"

A voice higher in pitch than mine, with a Long Island accent, said, "I'm an actor, man. An actor. Someone just wired me a lotta money and sent me this mask. They emailed me a tape to mimic. These clothes came this morning. They told me what to say. I memorized my lines. I do Off-Broadway stuff, dude. They said you'd get a kick outa this. That it was some big joke. I don't know, man. I don't!"

I rolled off. My impersonator bounded away with his mask half on.

I stood up breathing hard. I picked up the heavy blue binder with over six hundred pages of single type. I opened the cover and my eyes swelled.

On the front page there was a color caricature of a young Hardy Boyish–looking male stalking through a cyberworld with walls and floors made of 000s and 111s. The caricature had my physical characteristics. It looked like a Photoshopped image altered with filters and then toyed with in an illustrator program. The image had an expression of a homeowner looking for an intruder in the night. To my left and right were shadows of villains, the IRS, the FBI, and so many more. On my left foot was a ball and chain, only the ball wasn't a ball at all, it was my father's head.

Inside the folder was a table of contents of my life.

5

VERITY COMES CALLING

I LAY ON a couch in my Manhattan apartment that evening reading all about myself. Nothing was missed. From my birth certificate to my dental records to my school grades to my dozens of undercover jobs, it read like a resume to God. Not spun, tweaked, and exaggerated, but honestly, dutifully detailed. My fake identities, so carefully constructed, were simply listed as aliases. Carl Drucker, Nick Miller, Michael Waters . . . all the fools I'd created. There were even footnotes.

Amounts I was paid appeared with digital photocopies of checks. Account balances in banks in the U.S. and abroad were listed systematically. My IRS returns were in order. My Social Security contributions, credit score, and purchases, from the tennis racket I bought the month before to the wigs I'd bought to play another fake identity a year earlier, every purchase was listed on a timeline. The print was miniscule, single-spaced; the margins were filled with numbers, graphs accounting for funds and expenditures.

Emails, thousands of them, were printed in order. Replies were there too. There were highlighted links to audio, to phone calls I'd made, showing this was somewhere online. The websites I'd viewed were listed. Some embarrassing stuff there—a little porn showing my taste in women, some political articles I'd taken the time to read, even the books I'd purchased.

The criminals I'd busted were there too. Their mug shots were next to short bios. Lists of my employers, who my Facebook friends were, and hundreds of photos of me taken with cell phones in bars, at beaches, birthday parties, even of women I'd dated. Love letters, stupid, idiotic attempts at poetry to lovely Penelope were there. The eulogy I wrote and said at my mother's funeral when I was twelve, as well as some of the venting I'd done afterward; the blasphemy, the juvenile anger had been recorded and put there.

As were other stupid things I'd said in chat rooms, blogs, and things spoken and written while undercover, playing other people—hard-to-explain things there. As different characters I'd gone to strip clubs, to gay bars, had said things I'd didn't believe or think in order to stay in character, to bond with moles and bust them.

How do you explain the racial things, the sexist things said while playing Tony, a hooligan from the Bronx in order to bond with Victor, a hacker from the ghetto who lived in the shadow of Yankees Stadium and who was in organized crime, money laundering, insider trading? All the info was there, but who would read, grasp it all? All these things would be taken out of context, misunderstood. These were personal things, two-dimensional slices from a complex life. Seeing them all there systematically, flatly listed brought out all the personal scenes, the feelings flooded back as my memory filled in the stories, the contexts, some forgotten, others repressed.

My head spun. I cried. I cringed. I laughed. I blushed. I gritted my teeth.

I saw myself anew. Like watching yourself for the first time on TV, wondering is that really me? Is that really how I move, how

I sound? But knowing more, that your posture, hair, clothes, and more are all shields, parts of a developed image. What I saw in those pages bit me through the marrow. I saw myself, but I saw things I didn't recognize, traits I hadn't thought were there. I had a hard time comprehending this data.

I went from rage, to depression, and finally to acceptance over the course of hours of reading as night grew deep before succumbing to dawn. I just kept looking at my caricature and reading my personal thoughts and thinking wild, crazy things, remembering memories of my mother, friends, father and more. Heart-wrenching things . . . things that were only my business . . . things I regret . . . things I don't. Words spoken in anger, words said in lust.

Awful invective and insecurities said while a teen, when a twenty-something rising in a budding field. The time I grew arrogant after busting a hacker who'd been siphoning tiny fractions from millions of trades done on the New York Stock Exchange and stupidly told a trader I was the God in the details. "Oh, arrogance is such a turn-off," said a smart blonde to me in a Wall Street pub afterward. And I grew up then, some anyway. Now all these memories built atop other people's perceptions and really embarrassed me, really confused me. I was left with the impression I was a stranger to myself.

I crawled into bed on hands and knees. Exhausted.

I woke stiff. I was still dressed. A comforter was twisted around my body. I'd been rolling around from anxiety for how long? I saw my alarm clock. *Four? Still night. No, four p.m. on Wednesday?*

As I lay in a state of semi-consciousness, like a man knocked out in the ring who gets up not knowing he'd been out for much more than the ten seconds it takes to lose, I heard someone knock on the door. For a long moment I thought the sound came in a dream.

I sat up. Yes, I'd heard something.

No one knows this address . . . stupid, everyone knows now.

I peered through the peephole. Saw no one. Wondered a long moment. Opened the door an inch. Saw a package. Thought of running down the hall to the street to grab whomever had knocked. But I knew it was much too late.

I picked up the box and brought it inside. I pulled open the box, then sat back, with my eyes searching, thoughts scrambling. There was a note and an iPhone, a headset, and Google Glass Explorer Edition with some extra electronics wired into them.

I read, wondered out loud, "Verity wants me to go to the clock at the information booth in Grand Central Station at 6:00 p.m. And I'm to wear these glasses wired to this iPhone?"

I hurried into and out of the shower and dressed. My stomach felt sick. My heart was going too fast. I hit the PLB's button. I guessed this would get Special Agent Bent or whoever moving. It would get them following me, watching for Verity or something.

I hoped they'd nail the bastard who'd profiled me and that all this would be over. But I stopped myself from hoping too much, as I didn't trust the FBI. I didn't think they'd really just give me my old life back. No I was pretty sure they'd want something. I'd probably have to buy my freedom by working for the NSA. Maybe it would even be a Godfather kind of favor and I'd never know when they'd call on me to return the good turn.

I took the iPhone, headset, and glasses and left my laptop on a desk. I pulled on a hooded sweatshirt and left the building as cautiously as a deer creeping out of a cornfield at dusk. I looked at every passing face and compared them to memories of the people I'd busted. There were a lot of people on the sidewalks. No one was paying attention to me. Everything seemed normal. I walked along and pushed my hands into my sweatshirt's pockets and went down cement steps into a subway station. I waited while leaning against a tiled beam and kept looking too much at all the unsavory characters in the subway terminal. A train stopped. I got on and rode the clattering subway to Grand Central Station.

I walked up out of the subway terminal and onto Grand Central Station's main floor while watching thousands of faces rushing to trains. Every now and then a runner came through with his briefcase swinging, back arched, tie bouncing, running heel-to-toe, stopping only to glance at the board to see which track to dash for.

I lingered under the station's green ceiling, a planetarium of constellations. The room hummed with thousands of voices, hard soles stepping on marble, giving it a constant vibration of accents and dialects behind the drumming of a thousand heels—an appropriate background music for a city famous for its pace. I stood at the center by the clock atop the information booth. It read 5:58 p.m.

My eyes searched through a pair of amber-colored Google sunglasses wired to an iPhone with a headset. Other than a note reading, "Be at the information booth on the floor of Grand Central at 6:00 p.m., wear this device, and wait," and signed "Verity," there was nothing else in the box.

The glasses made everything look sepia-toned, only brighter, like a cartoon, but too heavy on the orange. So many people from all walks streamed past, lingering, meeting friends, family, bumping into one another almost as randomly as an old-style electric football game, the type with the magnetic floor that vibrated and the players danced and collided.

Then the second hand came around the nine and was turning up to the minute and hour hands.

Where's the FBI? Are they lingering in the eddies of the current of commuters? No, don't look. Being watched.

Static. Back feed. My hands went cold, numb. Is this Verity? A voice spoke from the headset, "Hello, Sidney."

The tone was deep, flat, barely an intonation, almost without accent. Altered by a computer?

Heart pounding, feeling like a secret agent who'd been found out, I replied almost calmly, "Good day. What can I do for you?" What do you say when you know it will be analyzed syllable by syllable by the government?

"I've bought you here to teach you and to meet you. You are an invisible thing, I must say. That's good. You're smart. Squeeze the bridge of your glasses, Sidney."

I did as instructed and words began to appear on the left when a reticle, a gray square, passed over people's faces. The words were people's ages, occupations, habits, more. I began to place the reticle on people. When they were close enough and I held it on them for long enough, photos, information flashed past as quickly as they did.

"Before the show starts, I need to teach you a few things. First appreciate the color, the particular shade of the glasses. They're highly polarized to cut out the haze, and are a crisp pleasant, bright color, like the leaves on a red oak in autumn. How does this make you feel?"

"Happy. It's like watching a cartoon."

Verity continued in a monotone, "Good, yes, exactly. A cartoon. Before you are many characters. Thousands of them. Playing their parts, their roles. Seen like this, the scene seems more perfect; it's less brutish than the spectrum God gave us. Now center the reticle on any person. There is a camera in your glasses frame; it's picking up each person's facial dimensions and linking it to their profiles. Forgive the mistakes and gaps, technology has a few more years of want in this category. Can you get readings? Not all of the people have profiles, yet. You have to center it right on someone's face, so it can get their facial dimensions."

"Yes, when they get close enough, and face me for long enough."

"Fine. What do you see?"

"Their actual face on the right lens of the glasses, on the left I see a caricature of them with their information streaming by."

"Good. Now you are looking at Gloria Shiller. Keep it on her a minute. She's waiting in front of the clock for her husband, as she does every day. Notice the simplicity of her, as you say, caricature, but I say soul; it's as simple as she is. No real differences. She's a happy, plain office worker, a content mother; she has a simple husband, and little mirth. Short slightly in the IQ, and maybe a little bereft of ambition, but happy, and true to her soul. She's rare. And she's useful."

"Now do you see the man in the leather coat leaning against the ticket window? The Italian with the eyebrows that look like a sweatband."

"Yes. Vito."

"Yes exactly. Look at his profile. Vito is a tradesman, a plumber. He's another rare example. And he's also useful."

"Useful?"

"To society."

I noticed one of the agents who'd grabbed me on the street. The man was moving through the crowd wearing dark slacks and a black sweater that he'd just bought from the Banana Republic just outside on 42nd Street. He stalled a little too much to look around.

"Go ahead and put the camera on the agent's scowling face," said Verity.

I tossed my head around.

"Come on, Sidney, put the camera on the man with the Banana Republic tag sticking from his pants."

I conceded, saw a caricature of a surly figure with the scheming expression of someone who's plotting something petty. His face was Special Agent Bent's, but the features also resembled a rat's. His body was gray and slouched, yet too dark to see details. It was the stooping posture, the withdrawn position of his arms and hands, and the raised upper lip under beady, bloodshot eyes that made the agent look like vermin.

Verity said, "Agent Jason Bent is not true to anyone, including himself. He idolized his father, who was a bad drunk and prone to angry outbursts for no rational reason at no rational time. His parents' marriage only lasted into Bent's teens because his father traveled constantly and beat his wife habitually. When he finally retired from the FBI, after only twenty years in, because his stomach was being eaten away by ulcers, his wife, Bent's poor mother, only stood his wrath for ten hours before moving into her lover's, the next-door neighbor's, home; however, Bent still idolizes his father, who died shortly after his divorce of gross unhappiness found in the bottom of bottles. Bent was an unpopular, arrogant youth, a sometimes tantrum-throwing student, and now a rat gnawing his way to the top. Bent has never learned to follow his own vision to achievement. He's always on the back of another, sticking knives in the fool carrying him whenever necessary to gain a better hold. He sold his soul to attain power. Bent decided Machiavelli's posthumous work *The Prince* is his guide in life. Bent has been on his dark, scheming path so long there's little real left of him. He'll never find inner peace. He'll never be comfortable with himself. He'll never be true to himself, because he's been twisting himself into a rat since grade school. He's never been, and he'll never be, useful."

During Verity's monologue Bent turned red as he moved off the station's floor.

I placed the floating square on an old man moving through with a cane. The man had a humped back, a mustache so long it framed his mouth, a bald head shaped like a cauliflower, and a gray suit stretched over his body's bumps and appendages.

Verity said, "*Hmm*, Harry Morton. He looks like he has a story to tell, but let's look deeper. Yes, just as I thought, it's harsh, common, and simple. His elder brother inherited the family practice and Harry has spent the last forty years being perverted by envy. Let's move on, he's worse than being useless; he's an anchor heavy with spite who never freed himself from the anger long enough to be a productive person pursuing happiness."

The flood of people kept streaming by and I picked out another character, a tall black man walking on the balls of his feet, bouncing above every head like a log caught in the current that won't sink.

Verity sounded disheartened, "This one's nicknamed 'the Raven.' He pushes large gray carts full of goods all day long on Park Avenue heckling people as he goes. He has learned to fit into his current occupation, but would have been better suited if he had become the fireman he longed to be. He'd say prejudice stopped him; I call his roadblock mislabeling, but it amounts to the same thing. He's been told his whole life that he is unintelligent, simply because he was born with a lisp; his palate's too big for his tongue. It's all there on your screen. From his high school guidance counselor telling him that he is not college material, to his friends and even girlfriends judging him by that lisp and berating him down to knee level. He could have been better used. Without the killing of his strong will by so many, I'm sure he would have overcome any racist gatekeeper at the fire department.

"Point those glasses around, nine out of ten of these characters aren't remotely true to themselves or even their roles, and this is mostly a professional crowd at this hour; commuters, people that can afford a house in the 'burbs. You wouldn't believe what you'd see if I took you down to the Port Authority, where the Jersey busses come in."

I continued looking at people and their caricatures. I could do this all day. Some surprised me, such as a grandmotherly-looking woman who sold heroin. She'd blown her chance on Broadway by living life too loosely.

A friendly-looking man who beat his wife for getting pregnant disgusted me. This selfish rogue hadn't wanted to marry, but loneliness and a pretty woman swooned him.

An angry-looking youth in clothes nine sizes too large really surprised me. This one had strait As and planned to go to medical school.

And all of these people had caricatures that matched the truth about who they were.

I asked, "How do you make so many caricatures . . . I mean souls?"

Verity said, "It's a simple computer-drawing program that uses real information from their profiles to create their soul's reflection. Simple logic gives the computer choices that it works through using mathematical variables; something Aristotle started but couldn't complete, a mathematical definition of human logic. I'll explain all of this another time, but really, it's very simple. Facial-recognition software uses photos from Facebook, Pinterest, Instagram, from high school yearbooks online, and so on. It then tweaks the photos according to their truth. All the information is on the net. Much of it is quietly being used by corporations to market to you and by the government to do more than you might yet believe. Much of this information is taken directly from data-mining corporations, legal companies that are now selling personal information on all of us. They're clumsy now, but are quickly, covertly, profiling everyone. Soon they'll say it's for our own good. They'll say we need to have the cameras on the corners and profiles of every citizen to nab the criminals to go along with national ideas loaded with biometrics. And that'll only be the beginning. Tyranny will follow.

"Be quiet now, the show is about to begin."

Twenty seconds of silence was filled with me pointing the glasses at people and marveling. Some had more info available than others, but only a few didn't have some kind of profile.

Verity interrupted my fun by saying, "Now watch. See the tan trench coat with the mustache and Stetson? Yes, that's right, Alex Morris. Keep your eye on that character. Look at the reflection of his soul. He's from a proper New England family. A family that inherited wealth from a nineteenth-century entrepreneur who manufactured shoes and in the generations since lost the morality that comes from earning your own bread. Alex wanted to marry Laura Roberts, his high school sweetheart, but he made the mistake of obeying his mother, and so married Jennifer Thomas, a woman with position, but scorn. He would have been disinherited the other way, but arguably happy. However, he took what he thought was the easy road. Now three decades of bearing the knowledge that another man is married to his love later, and watching her forget about him, while she raised a fine family, he is filled with hate. He wasn't true to his soul. This unhappiness has affected his business. He drinks too much. He isn't pleasant to be around. His investment firm, once prosperous, has all but dried up because of his regret, his self-loathing. His wife, whom he despised, continued to spend as she always did. Desperate and facing bankruptcy, he did the unthinkable. Watch."

Ten seconds passed and then screams echoed through the huge hall: "Murderer! Murderer!"

The angry shouts came from a childlike-looking man who was the size of a baby elephant. He had the round face of an infant, and the waistline of a sumo wrestler. He was wearing a green sweat suit and had unkempt brown, knotty hair that looked like it had just been resting on a pillow. The man-boy came striding heel-to-toe around the information booth hollering, "You killed my auntie! You smothered her with a pillow. Murderer!"

As the man-boy's screams echoed off Grand Central's planetarium ceiling, I placed the camera on the man-boy and found he was Alex Morris's nephew, a sometimes mental-facility occupant.

I read data streaming over my glasses and found that this man's nephew, Dean, was away at his anger-management class when Morris killed his wife. Morris foolishly admitted as much to a psychiatrist who gossiped about it to a colleague in California online, thereby creating a digital record, which Verity somehow copied and forwarded to this man-boy.

I refocused my eyes on the scene as the juvenile leviathan in a sweat suit grabbed Alex Morris by the arms and began shaking him like a man might a child.

"My auntie didn't die the first time, so you smothered her again," bellowed the man-boy's voice throughout the theater-sized station.

Alex succumbed to blind panic. His life had been reduced to his lowest moment. The truth had caught him.

Then a fist caught him. Another.

And cops were on the scene trying to pull them apart.

Morris lost all control of himself then. As he was being hit he was watching the woman he married for money, and later learned to loath, die so horribly under a pillow. He began to blather as the man-boy began to choke him, "I did it. I did it."

Tasers aimed from feet away shot thousands of volts into the man-boy. First one, then two, and finally three officers hit him until he was standing, shaking and jolting and finally falling to the marble floor.

The cops tossed glances at each other in amusement that it took enough juice to knock over a horse to subdue this lunatic.

But before the moment lapsed, the murderer continued to confess, "I killed her. I killed her; I did, I did . . ."

Then the man who killed his wife writhed on the floor and looked up at the constellations on the station's ceiling and thought he was looking into the void, to the place of judgment and he wanted to confess all his sins, yes, that was his plan, right at the last moment he'd just repent all his sins and everything would be all right.

His desperate confession caused the New York cops to shrug. They didn't care. But now they'd have to file reports, to investigate. All they really cared about was not getting his blood on their skin. But some district attorney would certainly love to take this man down.

It took two officers to roll the man-boy onto his back and to make sure he was still breathing.

With the fight over, I asked, "How did you set this up?"

"You think this was hard to orchestrate?" Verity asked with the same emotionless monotone. "People are so predictable. Alex Morris passes here during the same minute of every day to catch the 6:21. People have to learn that the roles they live are just that, roles. You choose your part or parts and you must pick them purely, on the basis of your character, and you must change roles as you develop, while keeping true to yourself along the way. People must learn this, and to then love their roles, to play them well. We're all actors on the earthy stage. That is what I do. This murderer needs to be taken out of society—he was fed up with playing a fake for a husband; he should have been truer to his soul by following his heart; he may not have succeeded, but he would have felt more fulfilled. He must now pay for his sins, his untruth, or his soul will never be saved."

Then speaking, enjoying his own dogma, Verity said, "God is said to judge all when they enter Heaven. Why wait? Let's bring Heaven down to Earth. Let the truth be seen and heard here and now.

"After all, the happiest are the purest. This is exhibited in works of art, whether they be photos, paintings, poems, or plays. If they portray the image, or sound, or event at the core and its message and stay in harmony, they become perfect capsules of life—the *Mona Lisa* is this. Life is an ever-changing thing; moments of perfection are always fleeting. The moment comes and it is perfect for but a moment before it's stepped on with some foul act or change in the weather. This is why we must change with it. Living our roles truthfully when they come and then changing fluidly when they change. This is what I do. And this is what I will teach the world through repentance. 'To thine own self be true, and it must follow as the night the day, thou canst be false to any man.' *Hamlet*."

Verity paused to draw a deep breath all the way to the bottom of his diaphragm, then said, "People need to find their roles from within themselves. Every infidelity or crime represents a lie, a departure from their true selves. Did you ever notice how people are very representational of their looks? The FBI agent to your left has the confidence of training and muscles, but not of acting. He feels insecure in his sweatshirt and baggy jeans. He's not completely comfortable with his role. Most of the exceptions are the strong-willed, because they've ignored society's pressure and found their roles despite others' views and biases.

"Sidney, I want to wipe out the 'isms': agism, sexism, racism, favoritism. I realize it isn't possible to wipe them out entirely, but it is possible to make them a much smaller variable. No longer will we be judged by color, size, or looks. We'll be judged by actions and thoughts. The truth will set us free!"

I broke in: "The whole truth and nothing but the truth, as in all trade secrets, all personal information whether it be medical or criminal, and even the secrets of our intelligence agencies open to everyone?"

"You go too far. I'll explain all of that another time. You're a curious little accomplishment of the American system, aren't you? This freedom to be who you want has helped prepare this nation for the steps to perfection. So many nations don't even have a free press to feed them half-truths. But to ease your worries, yes, all public figures need to be known fully. In time this will become their choice, if they run for office, then they choose the public scrutiny. The private citizen will have the choice to give his or her profile to employers, universities, and so on. And these institutions or people will have the power to ask for them or not. All should be as open as we want it to be. But for all government positions, the people must know everything. In time the practice will become accepted and the private sector will embrace it as well. But all state secrets and the like of course should remain in the vetted hands. It's just that those hands will be chosen more properly.

"Right now the government and industries are quietly watching us. And they're getting better at it. I think it would be better if we were watching them. If this march to government control continues George Orwell's *1984* will seem prophetic before another generation grows into fools."

Verity paused, said, "Government, of course, is clumsy, but it does keep stumbling forward. So really, I've just beaten them to profiling Americans by using the information they're gathering on us against them. This is why we need to kill Big Brother by shedding light on him. This is why I developed the system, the thing that builds the profiles you viewed this evening. This is why the Truth Seekers have been outing public officials—oh, you don't know about all that, do you? Some of the scandals have come out, and a few of them have even been publicly attributed to me, but they've kept it pretty quiet. They're hoping to make it through this election before they have to answer questions. The government is gaining control.

"Now, I know you want to ask about the system, and how all of this is possible—don't. I can't tell you at this time because Big Brother is listening. Instead, just imagine a world where criminals fear to tread, because breaking laws will also make you eligible for total exposure. A world where each individual is rewarded for their true abilities. A society where every individual is in total control of his or her own profile. Our bureaucratic system will no longer be able to eat the meek."

Verity took a breath, said, "Sidney, look into your mind for the true path. You need time to reflect. You need to be purged of the rest of the filth you've picked up in this society. You'll hate me, but then you'll find you're free. When things get bad ask yourself one question, ask your heart, your gut, and soul, 'Do I feel better or worse?' Deep down, it knows the truth."

Car horns came over the headset and Verity said, "Yes, Rooney, that's right, I was actually in the building." Then laughter and the boast, "You've failed again, Rooney, you Rottweiler of a human being. Sidney, you'll continue to be judged for all your sins. You'll overcome them when you use honesty, truth as your weapon. Soon you'll meet your guide to freedom. Good luck."

Silence then. The glasses blinked off. The connection to the system terminated.

I wandered confused out of Grand Central Station and across 42nd Street. I fell deep into the conundrum of wondering whether Verity was right.

6

THE ADVANTAGE OF
EVERYDAY LOOKS

THE SUN WAS just gone and the lampposts on along Park Avenue. People didn't look the same. They had the same fast strides and dark, fashionable clothes, but I kept seeing their dirty secrets, as if those Google glasses were still showing me their profiles.

I turned west on 38th Street and kept walking until I glanced left and locked eyes with a stranger. I was staring into my reflection in a deli's window. As I looked at myself, not one of my fake parts, I found I really didn't know myself. This guy in the reflection was young, thin, and so damn clueless he seemed to be begging for Hamlet's tragic end. Straight eyebrows, frosty hair, a forgettable nose, eyes resembling faded blue bulbs on some old strand of Christmas lights, a posture much too straight, a mouth held indifferently . . . Had I developed this identity according to my looks? What if I had a hatchet-shaped nose, buckteeth, and a bulbous forehead, or what if I was black, brown, or green? Would I be a different person? Would I think differently?

Maybe in some ways, naturally, but what about down deep where the something that is you projects from? Would my belief system, my intellect, my likes and dislikes, my worldview, my disposition, all the things that make me uniquely me, be different if my looks were? I didn't know. I thought perhaps Verity did. Or did he? That's a question I'd have to answer, somehow.

I was in an image-stricken society with people addicted to Botox injections, spray-on tans, and cosmetic surgery to improve self-image, yet I'd never really thought deeply about my own looks. I'd spent a great deal of time considering other's appearances, especially women's, but had never really understood mine even as I hid myself in undercover costumes. I'd always seen my physical image as a blank canvas, but never really considered its pieces in the raw, even as the sum of their genetic parts. Was that because they fit in so well, so commonly in this society? I had such an easy face, a countenance in this culture that enabled me to be transparent, to be attractive but not too much. I wondered if I was good looking. I wondered if, because I was so transparent, that I'd been easily able to become who I was on the inside. Or was I?

Then a sudden movement inside caused me to refocus my eyes through the deli's window. I was suddenly staring into narrow brown eyes hovering over a not-so-white T-shirt with sweat stains washing down from armpits.

I smiled back at the deli worker, before spinning around and walking away while wondering whether I would like to see Verity caught or left free. I was uncertain if I should join or fight the so-called Truth Seekers. I knew I had to pick a side, as not choosing was choosing.

Finally, I began to wend my way home. As I did I kept seeing FBI agents. Sometimes the one named Bent, sometimes others. I stopped in a Gap and left the store as a baggy pants–wearing youth with a bandana over my hair and an attitude in my stride.

When I slipped out of the store I saw an FBI man rushing around inside.

I put my phone's ear buds in and let my iPhone sing hip-hop into my ears. I strutted more than walked. A block from my apartment I began to pay attention to every sound, to inspect every face. I felt like a wildebeest approaching a watering hole knowing lions were somewhere in the tall grass.

The side street always had a person or two walking, hanging out or something, no matter the hour. It was part of the reason I chose this apartment. Too few people killed anonymity. Too many meant I couldn't spot the character who didn't belong. This time I saw a van that I'd never seen before. I guessed feds. Closer to the door to the building were two men standing apart, loners looking uncomfortable, uncertain. They stared at me too much. They didn't seem natural. They were amateurs.

I exaggerated my stride to the hip-hop's beat. As I passed the van I banged on its side—*boom, boom, boom*. I heard something fall inside, someone curse. I repressed a smile.

The two men waiting outside the apartment building came into focus in the living air on that cool fall night. But they just watched me swipe my card to unlock the door and strut inside the private building. One started to say something, but stopped when I started to sing, "It's bigger than hip hop, hip hop, hip hop, hip. It's bigger than hip hop, hip hop, hip hop, hip hop."

The door shut behind. I'd recognized one of the stooges waiting to wallop me, an information-services specialist I'd busted for stealing company funds a year before. I thought the guy had gotten three to five, but then white-collar crime is never taken seriously by the legal system.

The other didn't look familiar. I had done enough jobs by then to forget some, especially the ones who wear suits to the office to fit in, then morph into their street attire, their real personality's dress, street side.

I stepped off the elevator and used my phone to log on to my security system. I found the heart monitor in my apartment didn't read an intruder and the security hadn't been tripped. I went in knowing this would be my last night there. I could never come back. My Fortress of Solitude had been found. I'd been foolish to come this last time. I'd have to slip out with what I could carry. Maybe vanish. Maybe play another part. Be someone else. Never be myself, ever again.

But such decisions would have to wait. I must sleep. In the morning, with the sun, I'd decide.

I remembered reading that sick children are often at their worst in the hour before sunrise but when the sun peeks in their lives again fevers break, sanguinity resets. I hoped so.

7

ON THE RUN FROM HIMSELF

MY OUTLOOK SEEMED more desperate, more vivid when daylight came peeking over the Atlantic Thursday morning.

I stuffed a laptop, emergency cash, the blue binder recording my life, and some clothes in a fashionable commuter bag. I dressed smart casual, not knowing where I might need to fit in. I took a long look in the mirror. I thought I should stop looking in mirrors. Maybe forget what I look like long enough to define myself by my inside, by my soul or whatever was there, not my skin color and facial proportions. I thought that maybe Verity was right about that much, at least. After all, I didn't know how much of myself, or my understanding of myself, was defined by what stared back and how much was defined by what stared out. I thought I couldn't know unless somehow I shirked my reflection for a long time. Maybe I could train myself to only look at a small piece of myself at a time, to look at and fix first one part of my hair and then another and then my mouth, nose . . . to only see parts and thereby forget the whole. Would that give me freedom from my reflection? Was that what Verity did?

I shook my head and knew I was spiraling down into a black hole of unknowns. I couldn't decide if Verity was right, or rather, how much he was right.

I put the bag's strap over my head, around my body, and stepped lightly out of the apartment and went down ten flights of stairs to the street. I stopped. Waited. I watched people on the street through a small window in the door from the stairs that looked into the lobby. I recognized some, even saw Victor, the Bronx hoodlum I'd befriended and busted. Victor was wearing his usual baggy jeans and winter coat that looked like it had been inflated with an air compressor.

I went back upstairs to the roof. The sky was a cold blue, crisp autumn air wafted a hint of decaying leaves from somewhere far, far west. Horns blasted below. I could feel the movement of millions of people like the vibrations of speakers, all the world seemed small and endless all at once below and about me.

I jumped, landed on a building a story below. Heard feet on stone. Turned. Saw two people coming. Began to run, to jump.

"You, you, Carl or Sidney or whatever the fuck you call yourself. You cost me everything."

Down a fire escape . . . sprinting along a street . . . diving into a subway . . . really running then . . . up onto the street again and around a block. Lost them, lost them . . . no . . . an arm grabbing mine . . . I spun, slipped, landed on asphalt cradling my laptop.

A paper was shoved into my chest as a voice from gasping lungs beneath a sweaty suit snarled, "You've just been served, Sidney McDaniel."

I stood right into a taxi. Someone was pounding on the yellow roof. The driver hit the gas while screaming Hindu or something and then blocks blurred passed.

"Where to?"

"Columbia University."

Though just past thirty years old, I still had to show my ID every time I bellied up to a bar, so I fit seamlessly with the students at Columbia.

An hour passed before I felt sure I hadn't been followed. I found a seat in a student café. I sat on a plastic chair at a small, round table. I opened my laptop and logged on to a wireless connection I knew I'd find there. I thought maybe I could check my computer's ports and hard drive and find some intrusion, some clues. I fell back to my skills and slipped into the digital world. I began reading code and using intrusion-detection software as the software sniffed for tracks leading in and out. I hunted for spyware. Hours passed. I wasn't finding malware or invasions of my system. I thought it unlikely they'd hacked me, but how else could they know so much? My security was tight, so I thought they must have gotten my personal info by siphoning it from routers, from third parties, even though that would take an uncommon amount of access.

I checked my email accounts again and saw they were still filling with comments, angry and friendly, from my past and present.

I stayed aware of the people moving around me, so I saw her right away. Though I'd have seen her coming anytime. She wore what had to be ludicrously expensive heels that clicked on the tile floor with a confident rhythm. She wore a black business suit with pants that were both professional and tight enough to reveal her ballerina figure. She had strawberry blonde hair and a youthful glow. She was feminine in an age when so many American women thought they needed to be masculine, at least by day. She managed to embody that living contradiction only a few women accomplish: she was sensuously animated yet untouchably statuesque, sexy yet strong.

Then she was there looking not at me, but into me.

I felt goose bumps grow.

Her voice whispered loud from five feet away, "Hi Sidney."

I coiled to leap, to run.

"Don't be alarmed," she said as she sat down across from me. "You don't know me, but you might know everything, someday."

I fell into her sharp hazel eyes.

She smiled wonderfully and said with a light, friendly intonation, "My name's Aster."

She reached out her hand and I shook it foolishly—she was too beautiful for a young man to treat casually.

She let go of my hand and slipped a USB port into my laptop. It began downloading something. I moved to rip it out, but she took my hand again.

"It's okay," she assured as she crossed her legs and smiled.

A file popped onto my desktop.

"Open it."

I thought to trash it, to run away, but something about her sure, relaxed manner seduced me into opening the file.

My profile opened. But there was also info on who was investigating me—the IRS agent with my case file, legal precedents, more.

"Huh?"

"I'm an attorney. I represent the Truth Seekers. Well, not publicly." She smiled and said, "You can free yourself with the truth. Your accounts have been locked. You can now unlock them. A DA is filing charges. You can now show him there's nothing there but spin. All you have to fear now is yourself. Have you done something you can be punished for? Something you can't handle paying for?"

"Um, no, I've . . ."

"That's the question you'll have to answer. This is your choice. You can fight back with all the truth and you'll win if you're right, if you're clean. But you must first know that using the system, the truth, is joining us. Do so and I'll find you again. Bye."

She stood and turned and I watched her figure slip away as her hips moved just a little more than necessary.

I didn't even think of following, of demanding answers, retribution.

This was all too much.

8

THE DOUBLE-EDGED SWORD

I SAT IN the student café reading everything. I found freedom in the documents. And blackmail. The IRS agent with my case file and the DA filing charges were guilty of fraud, graft, and infidelity. I could stop them easily. By staying honest, even when undercover, I had stayed free of their tentacles, of their guilt, of things that could be used to make a person sink down into the mire of serious illegality. I was sure that if you profit from illegality then others will tug you all the way in, as the guilty abhor the honorable; they want others to wallow with them. Staying clean is the only way to stay free from their grimy little grips.

No, these authority figures couldn't do much to me. I was clean of anything serious. Creating the false identities was really the worst thing I'd done. There was enough there, in the hands of a savvy public prosecutor anyway, to give me hefty fines and community service. But I doubted any DA would take the time to build the case. These were trivial crimes. And they were complicated. It would be a waste of public resources to bring me to court. At worst my guilt would be plea-bargained away to fines.

Verity said government workers should have their profiles made public? Yes. According to Verity's code this is right, it's using truth to kill Big Brother. And now if I do, I'll be implicated. I'll be joining them.

This information was my savior and damnation. But what choice was there? I could take flight and give up everything as I ran from everyone and tried to start over, though I'd never again be able to run an undercover computer forensics company—at least not a legal one. Or I could stay and use this info and join Verity.

This was what that FBI agent, Rooney, wanted, wasn't it? Me on the inside. Me to join the Truth Seekers and then to wait for the FBI to contact me.

Yes, I didn't have a choice; I had to keep playing a pawn, for now.

I pulled my cell phone out. Dialed.

"Is this District Attorney Al Lebowitz?"

"What? Yes. How did you get this cell number? This is a private number."

"I'm Sidney McDaniel."

Silence.

"You have my case."

The DA exhaled, "*Uh-huh*."

"I'm sending an email to your personal account right now. In it you'll find that all my jobs were legit. Each is there in black and white. I also have videos of every person from every company who ever hired me saying such. But if you insist on going to court there will be more. See the attachment marked 'Lebowitz's Graft' and the other marked 'Lebowitz's Call Girls.' There are videos. One I found quite good. She should be a gymnast."

Long seconds of silence ended with a sigh formed into the syllables, "You're blackmailing me?"

"No, just demanding justice. Are you going to drop the charges?"

"Well, I . . ."

"I can email the *Wall Street Journal* as easily—"

I heard Lebowitz clicking attachments before gulping out the words, "Yes, yes . . . as long as you're innocent you have nothing to fear from us naturally, I mean—"

"Goodbye."

My next call was to the IRS agent who was assigned my case file.

The woman was courteous and helpful and really didn't want her record of especially targeting good-looking single men for full audits to be brought to the attention of her superiors.

All my funds were to be unfrozen. I was getting my life back a battle at a time. Or was I shackling myself all the more?

9

THE GATHERING

I WALKED INTO the Citibank at the Chrysler Center that Thursday afternoon. I withdrew thousands of dollars in small bills. Tellers in starchy shirts watched me curiously. A manager who spoke with the quiet, penetrating monotone a mortician prefers, asked if everything was all right.

"Yes, fine, fine." I acted impatient, as busy, perturbed people seem smart and important and hard to approach; I really didn't want to answer anyone's invasive questions.

I withdrew enough money to live on for a while and then walked back out onto the Manhattan streets. I rode subways north and west and stashed some cash in a locker at the Port Authority. Run away money. Cash left at a major bus terminal I hoped I'd never need. I bought a travel wallet from a street vendor outside, the kind of wallet that attaches to a belt and rests inside your pants, the type of wallet Americans buy before they go to Prague. I stuffed it full of walking money.

I rode the subways again and found a room at the Hotel Roger Williams in Midtown at Murray Hill. I told the middle-aged woman at the front desk my wallet had been swiped, and with it all my credit cards, but that I'd kept my cash separate. The wrinkled prude in the wool skirt and frilly silk top didn't buy this lie. But I handed her $600 for incidentals and said I'd just be there for a few nights with my most plaintive look and she relaxed and decided I looked harmless and dressed well enough. Maybe she thought I just wanted to cheat on my wife. She gave me a room on the fifth floor.

I went up to a clean room stuffed with outdated furnishings and logged on through the hotel's wireless service. A window popped open on the laptop's screen that read, "Click here if you agree to the following terms. If you agree to live the truth and nothing but the truth; if you agree to defend the privacy of individuals; if you agree to make government transparent; if you agree that people should be the masters of their profiles unless they decide otherwise; if you agree to kill Big Brother. –The Truth Seekers"

There was a box at the end. I didn't hesitate. My decision had already been made. I clicked on it. The terms faded away.

Then there she was.

Aster's colorful caricature splashed across the laptop's screen. The image grown from her profile fit with the others Verity had shown me in Grand Central Station. Her caricature ("soul's image" as Verity referred to it) was a color photo of her tweaked to include bits of personality traits, a picture of who she really was inside. Only she didn't look encumbered by untruth, as most had, but rather like a superhero. She had red flowing hair, a body suit showing off a figure that belonged in a Japanese comic book, captivating eyes under smart-looking glasses that screamed she had superpowers. She was standing in front of the scales of justice, trying to physically stop Uncle Sam from piling paper onto one side of the blind woman's scale. She was a heroine fighting for blind truth.

I stared at her sensuous figure for a long minute before scrolling through her profile. Mother killed in a car accident when she was four . . . a deadbeat dad . . . a law degree from Columbia. Foster homes. Bad stuff there. Psychologists saying she had an "antisocial personality disorder," a "father complex." Single. Smart. Worked for a prestigious international law firm in Manhattan. Liked dogs, not cats, but didn't have either. Worked out an hour a day. Read all the classics, but loved cheap mysteries. Felt happiest in the ripe darkness of a movie theater. Voted independently . . .

As I read all about her, Aster's charming voice suddenly leapt out of my computer's speakers.

I jumped like a startled cat.

Then her face was there on my laptop's screen and she was laughing before she began speaking. "Hi Sidney. I've read your profile. Time you read mine. Glad you decided to embrace the truth. We're going to work together. And partners don't keep secrets from each other. It's part of the deal. Everyone knows one other person—that's all. This conversation is encrypted with an algorithm the NSA estimated would take seventy-seven years for all its computers to crack. So we're safe. I'm glad you've chosen the true path. Love the way the truth set you free?"

It was five seconds before I realized the question wasn't rhetorical. "Ah, yes."

"Good. No more online lies or your caricature's nose will grow."

I sat back down from where I'd jumped to and my composure returned enough for me to ask a dumb question as I waited for my mind to grasp this new reality: "Why the name Aster? Must be a cybername."

She said, "Sure, it's so much more appropriate than my given name. An aster is a flower, a delicate little flower with petals like a daisy's. My grandmother used to plant them. My real name's Nancy Coldworth, but people named Nancy wear plaid dresses and live in Kansas. And Coldworth makes me sound like a witch. Aster is who I am. Did you ever take a cybername?"

"I am sometimes Privateer," I said, knowing she already knew that and everything else. "You know the old sea captain who, like a mercenary, patriotically joined the navy to battle an evil enemy. Somehow the name just fit. But I'm wary now of any constant name. I find that it's more advantageous for a cybercop to be a chameleon. You know, take on different identities, names and such, to get people's trust as is necessary."

"I've seen. You've been deceitful."

"Security protection can be," I said. "I try to walk the line. But you know, the funny thing is, I never have to lie. People assume the most absurd things when you withhold the right information."

"How so?"

"Let's say I tell you I've written programs, that I like the dark side of the net, that I spend my off time fooling with systems. Am I cop or villain?"

"I understand."

"What about you? If you don't publicly represent the Truth Seekers, what do you do?"

"Oh, legal advice mostly. I'm an expert on privacy issues, or their lack thereof really. We stay within the boundaries of the laws; oh, sure we bend them, but we're always careful how far. It actually would shock most people to find out just how little privacy they really have. The laws just haven't caught up with the technology. I can legally get your Social Security number. I can legally monitor your emails and legally place programs, cookies or whatever, unbeknownst to you on your computer to watch everywhere you go online and everything you do. I can legally use this information to create a profile of you and then legally sell that information to anyone I want. I can find out what you paid for a house, get information on your personal status you've provided to Myspace or eHarmony. I can legally get your photo from the state or from your high school or from wherever. There is very little I can't legally do to watch, profile, and monitor you. And I can do all that without your knowing it. Corporations do this already. The government is getting better at finding loopholes to do this. The Truth Seekers are just ahead of the curve. But I make sure we stay legal. Oh, I can't say that everything we do is legit. I'm only consulted on privacy matters. But, as I said, you'd be surprised what is now legal in the United States."

"Yes, legality and morality aren't synonyms," I said, finding her so easy to talk to as the ice broke. "And you attorneys live on loopholes, don't you?"

She paused. Bit her lip. Then flashed all her teeth as she said, "Sidney, our conversations will get so much more interesting when you've read all about me. We'll be like two old friends who know everything about each other and so have private jokes. So read about me. Tomorrow we'll talk again. We have work to do. Oh, and be sure to be online at midnight. There's a gathering tonight."

"A what?" I asked, but she was gone.

Midnight struck as the calendar turned to Friday and even Manhattan seemed to be slumbering beneath cold twinkling stars.

My laptop woke.

Eyes flashed on the screen. Just eyes. Brown living eyes. Someone's glare was floating there on an otherwise black screen.

I felt pushed physically back.

Verity's digitally altered voice, the one I'd heard in Grand Central Station, said, "Relax, Sidney. I'm showing you my eyes, as I do the other members of the Truth Seekers. A wise person once said the eyes are windows to the soul. So I show you mine. And through them you see me, the real me, not the flesh, but the mind, the thoughts not spoken, the spiritual thing filtered through the physical body. This way you see me more purely, with less bias. This way your mind can fill in the details based on my truth. This way you can only know me by me."

I steeled my countenance. I knew I wasn't just looking at eyes, but looking into someone's eyes. I was being watched, judged. Likely programs were even reading my expression, watching for changes in eye dilation, in blood in my facial skin, reading the ever-changing positions of my mouth, the tilt of my head, and more, all to be calculated according to a baseline. I was being judged.

Verity's invasive glare left me and went up as a preacher does during a sermon and I took a breath as Verity began his homily.

"My children, we have another believer among us tonight. He will help us in this final hour."

"Your word is true," chanted a parish of altered voices.

I shivered.

Verity continued preaching: "We are nearing the beginning. The true system lives and grows. The masses are almost ready for the true message. They are beginning to see their statesmen for who they truly are. Soon they will see themselves for the first time. Criminals will be flushed out. All will feel the need to go to confession. Not in a private booth, where their faces are shielded and their identities hidden, but in public, openly and honestly; to their loved ones, and friends, enemies, and rivals. Those truest to their souls will prevail. Others will change. Some will be swept away. It will be a painful metamorphosis. But society will be stronger, because people will do what they are meant to and lost souls will be found by the truth."

"Your word is true," chanted his followers.

Verity kept sermonizing: "No longer will people rise with lies, twists of the truth, and by feeding off the worth of others. The shakeout will be immense. This you all know. I've gathered you here to tell you that the time has arrived for conclusive action. You've raided the servers used by government and industry to watch, catalog, and track private individuals and you've opened them up to our prying eyes. You've grown the system and made the truth unstoppable. Now you are being emailed your orders. Follow them closely. You need only await the sign to begin the movement. There are people in key positions in government and the media who will help you begin. Remember, victory comes from numbers. The establishment will attempt to defend itself. They will persecute me. But the true word will prevail. The power will return to the people. Preach the truth and know thyself. They will all be reading the truth soon. They are almost ready for you and for themselves. This election will be truer than any before."

"Your word is true," chanted the voices.

"Watch the news in the morning, my disciples of the truth. We have shed light on an attempt by a political party to use private credit card company data and state drivers' records as voter-mining tools. This was a secret agreement. This private data is the individuals'. They have no idea how much of what they say and do is being sold and used by our government and industry. They'll know more tomorrow. Go now and preach the true word. It is almost time to kill Big Brother on the alter of honesty."

"Your word is true."

Verity looked directly into my eyes again as he said, "Sidney and Aster raise your eyes. We are alone now. You two now know each other. You don't know all the rest. This secrecy is for your own protection, as it is for mine; one bad apple can't destroy all we've worked for. I have important missions for you. These next days will be hard. There will be casualties. We have all seen the beginning. I expect a lot from you."

"Your word is true," Aster and I said.

Verity's raping eyes faded off the screen but I still felt like I was being watched, so I turned off and closed the laptop and stepped back from it as if the PC was a mad dog sleeping. I went to bed while eyeing the laptop resting innocently on a small desk in the hotel room.

10

THE DOUBLE AGENT

I WAS STILL in bed when the morning commuters rushed onto the island that some tribe long ago parted with for $24. I could almost hear their shoes slapping along the sidewalks, could almost see their determined strides, set jaws as millions of them flooded on for another day, a Friday. I felt envious of them. They were hidden in the herd. I'd been cut out, made ready for slaughter.

I pulled the covers over my head and almost felt safe behind the anonymity of cash. I'd taken the battery from my cell phone, as it had an imbedded GPS device. And I'd taken the battery from my laptop. I felt like a paranoid nut, a conspiracy theorist caught in a delusion of government surveillance and control.

How could all this be happening? How could some system run by some online cult do all this?

I picked up a remote control and switched on the TV and saw a reporter snickering about a scandal. The presidential election was next Tuesday and Verity had uncovered politicians using credit-card records and more to profile voters in certain districts and to thereby send them targeted ads. Verity had emailed the info to reporters. The funny thing was, noted the journalist, different people received different messages. The talking-head reporter held up two. They were for the same candidate but held contradictory stances. This politician was not just telling people what they wanted to hear, he was telling individual voters what they wanted to hear. What was the world coming to?

There was more but I didn't want to hear. I got out of bed and approached my laptop. I touched it like I was waking a wild animal and expecting it to bite me. I put the battery back in. I opened it and turned it on. It fired up and there was Aster waiting, staring with a look of disdain only females truly master.

"Sidney, you have to keep your laptop open and on. You can't shut us off."

She was frustrated. Her eyes were hard, her lips taut. She'd been trying to get me for hours. She took a breath, said, "Okay, sorry. I realize you don't know all the rules yet. Get dressed. You look like you slept on the street. Meet me in forty-five minutes at the southeast corner of Chambers and Broadway."

"At city hall?"

"Hurry!"

I'd joined an army and was being sent to battle to fight for what I didn't know. I was subject to this army's authority, and to its goals, whatever they might be. I'd only be told what I needed to know, nothing more. I was the definition of a grunt, a pawn.

I didn't like being expendable for an agenda I didn't even know, much less was even certain I agreed with.

The steps of New York's city hall were covered with journalists as exuberant as a pack of hounds on the scent.

Aster and I stood together on a sidewalk just far enough away from the pack not to associate ourselves with them. As we waited for something to happen, Aster handed me her iPhone. I looked and my eyes went buggy. I scrolled down, bewildered. I saw all the journalists looking at their smartphones and noticed they were snickering; they were on the scent all right.

As I scrolled through the profile of New York City's mayor, Bill Perkins, Aster whispered in my ear, "Emails notified these reporters to be here an hour ago. We just sent them pieces of Mayor Bill Perkins' profile."

"They'll eat him alive," I said. The caricature was bad enough. Perkins, who already looked like Jackie Mason's short brother, was wearing an open bathrobe with a miniature blonde gal clasping his right leg and a brunette holding his left while his wife and children cried in the background. The image left nothing for the imagination to fill in.

I was too disgusted to continue reading and shifted my eyes to the scene and saw a lectern waiting on the sidewalk. The mayor was supposed to stand on the three-foot-high platform behind the lectern and give his weekly press conference. Each week he briefly touted some spun achievement or proposed a new program before taking questions. Mayor Perkins had run on a platform of transparency and this was the most visible indication of that campaign promise. His aids and security waited around the lectern. Other than their shiny Italian suits, what one noticed about them was their height, as none was taller than five foot, three inches, which just happened to be the mayor's height when wearing his specially heeled shoes. The mayor's first requirement wasn't ability, but simply: "They'd better not be taller than me!" After all, he understood image, and he wanted to appear tall and powerful despite his disadvantageous genetics.

Three types of journalists were in attendance. First there was the machine-gun nest of television cameras right up front where the mayor's car would stop. At the center of this proud group of correspondents and cameramen was none other than Oliver Wissel himself, the host of the cable talk show *The Witness Box*. These broadcasters wore white shirts, dark suits, bright ties, and wingtips. Their cameramen wore sweatshirts over bulging stomachs, sneakers, and had the personal hygiene of high school cafeteria workers. Next came the big newspaper print reporters and their photographers. They wore washed-out suits, frayed sport coats, spent leather shoes, and their ties dangled under unfastened buttons. Behind them were smaller newspapermen and bloggers, who looked pointedly disheveled in jeans and had cheap winter coats, and felt so debonair in their loser, anti-establishment dress.

Somewhere in the back a blogger was boisterously summing up what he was reading on his BlackBerry to three other bloggers. "Mayor Bill Perkins' real name is Wilber, though he went by 'Willy the Peeper' when he was in grade school. He was the kid who came to class with a *Hustler* he stole from a market so he could sell peeks on the playground. He earned his nickname at age eight when Ms. Evans, his third-grade teacher, looked under her desk to see what the ruckus was about, and found Willy looking up her skirt. Ha, he lost his virginity at twelve to Estelle Baker, a forty-two-year-old widow who lived across the street. He knocked her up. Of course she wanted the baby, only Willy's mother found out and chased the widow out of the neighborhood. Ha, and get this, the child is now a thirty-eight-year-old used-car salesman in Des Moines."

Minutes blew by as Sidney and all the reporters read the mayor's profile and jabbed each other with their elbows as they pointed to startling evidence and texted the funniest stuff to colleagues. Then a limo approached and the pack of journalists jostled for prime positions. They were hissing, "He's dirty. He hired pros. We've got him. He vacationed in a Vegas spa. He's had affairs . . . oh boy has he had affairs . . . he's had affairs on his affairs. Some were gifts from lobbyists . . . Look at the emails he sent to Representative Morey. He bragged about an eighteen-year-old. He has a daughter who's older."

Then there was the filler. The stuff only the bloggers in back would publish, but that they'd all gossip about: That he traded votes for a roll in the sack . . . that he bet on a woman's chastity . . . that he told an environmentalist with the Sierra Club if she took off her pants "he'd pay for her services with a vote to save the panda or green tree frog or whatever member of the food chain was next up in line."

And it was all sourced. There were recorded snippets of his private telephone conversations. Emails. Witnesses. Accomplices. Medical records. Expunged criminal records. Report cards. Records of abortions he'd paid for. Notes from closed meetings. It was all verifiable, second sourced, and undoubtedly factual.

The limo stopped. Mayor Perkins stepped out in his pinstriped suit and rose to five foot, three inches on his custom-heeled shoes. His mouth flashed his practiced politician's smile, then drooped under bewilderment as his diminutive assistants hustled to tell him something frightful was about to happen. Before they could usher him back into his car he was surrounded, cut off as cameras fired away and reporters lobbed grenades.

"Mayor," shot one, "do you have any comment about the call girls you've hired?"

With his face flushing and heart slamming the mayor's attention spun around as he stared straight at the mass of ravenous reporters.

"Mayor, is twenty-seven women in the last nine months an accurate count?"

"Mayor, did you really pay off a sexual-harassment suit with insider trading tips?"

The mayor blindly shoved his way through the biting crowd. His security detail tried to help, but were soon overwhelmed. His assistants were too puny to act as offensive linemen.

The mayor's hands shook, went numb. He saw the journalists as one animal, one large creature ripping at his exposed belly. He felt their fangs sinking into his flesh as they pounced, fell on his throat. He began to run. He tripped. He fell. No one helped him up. He rose to his knees, then his feet. A camera knocked against his skull. The creature was all around. It had so many heads, so many teeth, so many drooling mouths crying for blood, his blood, so many feet stepping all over him.

He broke free. Began to run, to run faster than his fat, little legs had in decades.

An assistant stood banally in front of the door—his escape—not moving.

Mayor Perkins shoved her aside.

The creature roared behind: "Mayor, do you have a comment . . . ?"

He went in the door, up the steps. The snarling creature slowed at the metal detector. Officers let Mayor Perkins through as they stood with baffled expressions.

Mayor Perkins ran into his office, pushed past a staring secretary. He slammed the oak door, locked a steel bolt. He shoved a chair in front of the heavy wood door. He stumbled, fell into his swivel chair. He dropped his face into his hands. His phone began to ring. Someone was knocking desperately on the door. He started to cry.

Aster was smirking in the morning sun as a child does after an innocent prank.

I looked at her seriously.

She saw my somber expression and blushed.

"He may have deserved that, but it's wrong to enjoy someone's downfall."

We began to walk together north along Broadway. We didn't speak for several blocks, then Aster said with a hint of melancholy washing out her tone, "Just toss your computer bag, laptop and all, in the next trash can. Take this one. We can't trust the one you're carrying. The NSA may be monitoring it. We've checked its files and it seems fine but we don't take chances. We change ours every other week as a safeguard. We buy them randomly."

I hesitated, then tossed the whole bag. There was nothing irreplaceable in the bag and it was all password protected and encrypted. It seemed somehow appropriate to trash the last semblance of my private self. I was in too deep. I'd have to take orders until I saw a way out, if there was a clean way out.

I took the new computer bag from her knowing it contained viruses and software that would watch and track me. I'd become a pawn in a movement I didn't yet comprehend. I wasn't free. I was a slave. The whole damn thing was too daunting to comprehend.

"The phone and PC in the bag are encrypted with things free from NSA trapdoors. We have just one rule: absolute openness and honesty with the Truth Seekers. Verity monitors us all the time. He directs us the way a general does troops. It's not perfect, but one day soon we'll be able to be honest with everyone; one day we'll take back our identities and kill Big Brother and then we'll all be able to know each other, to really meet one another."

She looked at me softly and said almost too quietly for me to hear, "Sidney, you're going to be a double agent. I'm to help you."

We didn't talk for a long time. We kept walking north, weaving through pedestrians and across traffic-filled streets. She began to speak again when we found a relatively empty sidewalk, "As you should know from my profile, I'm a privacy attorney. I'd like to tell you in my own words how I met Verity."

I nodded and she said, "I found out while in law school that my psych file had quietly followed and shaped my life, a file I wasn't allowed to legally see. So I began fighting to see my file. It detailed my foster-home parents, the abuse, the psychotherapy sessions, and so much more. The file shadowed me. It helped and hurt me, but always directed me. It was a file every authority figure got to read, but I couldn't see. I sued and fought them. The bureaucratic system protected itself. Doctors and bureaucrats didn't want to be judged, to be held accountable for their opinions. I finally won by using the old laws, the ones written before all this technology, when people still had real privacy. When I read my file I realized I wouldn't have gotten into some of the schools I did without the file labeling me as a special case. I also found that I was passed up for an internship at the DA's office because of the file's conclusions of my mental health, suppositions based on my foster-care background. I found that this thing, this file filled with other people's perceptions of me, was shaping my life and there was little I could do about it.

"That's when Verity contacted me. He told me I could help so many more to take control of their profiles, of their lives. Things like grade school IQ tests, guidance counselor opinions, recommendation letters, criminal histories, and more follow us, yet people don't have the right to see them. And even when they do, they often don't know whom to ask, or where to start. And this is only the beginning. This is now a networked world and Big Brother is just learning how to use this information."

I could understand all that. But I still wasn't sure whether Verity was right, though I was certain Verity wasn't all wrong. Even Aster was unsure. She was rationalizing, trying to convince herself, looking for me to validate her conclusions. I couldn't do that, not yet, not until I was sure, so I said, "Makes sense, I guess. I can understand all that anyway. But the rest of it, how can all this profiling, those caricatures and so on be right? I'm not saying they're wrong; I'm just saying I don't know."

Aster grabbed my arm and I felt her feminine fingers push their nails into my flesh as she said, "Sidney, you have to be careful. Verity is always listening, watching. You're in now. You can't talk like that."

I bowed my head as we walked slowly into a park as I rubbed my arm.

"Nice grip."

"Sorry."

I stopped, turned to her and said, "If he's right, if he's good, then what's to fear?"

She bit her lower lip, said, "Right and good are not synonyms either, Sidney. Besides, Verity has to use the truth, sometimes only part of the truth, to protect the movement. Don't cross him. Knowledge is power. But soon, the power will be in everyone's hands. Don't you see, the system is the only hope? This digital world is giving the government, giving big business, the power to watch and judge and use us in ways we're just starting to comprehend. We have to take control of our own information before it's too late, before we wake up in an Orwellian reality."

I needed to know more before I could debate the merits, the downsides, so I shifted to a question: "You said I'm to be a double agent. What did you mean?"

She took a long breath that heaved her chest and reset her bearing before explaining, "The FBI has been frantically looking for you. You did a good job slipping them yesterday. It was why I was able to come to you. Now Verity wants you to get picked up by them. It's all in your computer. We need you to convince them to take you to the NSA's HQ down near DC. We need you to meet the team that's hunting Verity. Tell them you have ideas how this could be happening. Tell them you have to talk directly to people who will understand the computer languages you're referring to . . . that it's the only way . . . that you don't know where the conversation will go. Tell them to take you there right away. Once inside . . . well, the instructions are there on your PC. Read them carefully as they'll erase five minutes after you open them."

11

TREASON

I WANDERED BACK between the rushing people along the fervid streets of Manhattan. I went into my small hotel room on the buzzing island. I closed my hotel room door as horns blared along the streets below. I turned a deadbolt and put on the door chain. I slowly blew the stench of this day from my nostrils.

After a long moment, I turned around and peered out the peephole. A young couple merrily talking about some Broadway show passed down the hall. I breathed, let my real self out as my guarded public mask fell away for a moment.

A minute later I slowly pivoted my body as I pulled the laptop bag off my shoulder and placed it on a small desk. I took out the laptop computer. I stepped back and looked at the PC as if it were a blood-and-flesh snitch. I took a moment to compose myself again as a news broadcaster does just before the green light pops on. I regrew my blank public mask. I turned on the new laptop.

The orders from Verity were simple, yet horrifying. Would I be a traitor? This was almost espionage. Maybe this was right, maybe it wasn't. I wasn't sure. I wasn't sure if this were legally wrong or in a gray area. But it morally felt wrong.

Somehow I managed to keep this fear and uncertainty off of my face. The message erased. I left the laptop open as instructed. I showered and dressed slowly as my mind stood back and looked over this dilemma. I didn't see a way out. I felt like I was playing a chess master who was guiding me a move at a time to checkmate, yet there was nothing I could do.

The phone Aster had given me had a GPS capability, as most do. Undoubtedly, Verity or his people tracked me with this. They'd know where I was within six feet everywhere they could get a satellite signal. I had to be careful. I had to be smart. I had to keep chasing this rabbit until . . . ?

I left my hotel room with my new phone on and laptop in the computer bag hung over my head and left shoulder. I felt like a prisoner wearing a security anklet who really just wanted to be one of the good guys, only I was beginning to believe there really were no good guys, that you only found such characters in Hollywood thrillers. I walked out of the hotel and found a sunny sky just visible up between high-rises. I went down the stairs into the nearest subway station and rode an underground train through the intestines of the city and walked to where I thought the brownstone the FBI had taken me to a very long two days before must be.

I leaned against a lamppost and waited as the sun arced orange over the street and people walked past. Four small sycamores dropped yellow leaves over autos as wind reached down and tickled them loose. I pushed the button on the PLB the FBI gave me.

Just ten seconds passed before four agents busted out of a building.

Agent Bent skid to a stop on the cement sidewalk when he spotted me casually leaning against a lamppost.

Bent began cracking his knuckles as he spoke into a Bluetooth.

I shrugged, started to walk away.

A minute later a black Suburban slowed beside me. A rear window came down. Rooney was sucking air through a cigar and glaring.

"Get in!"

I laughed. The power had shifted. Now they needed me. Now I knew more than they did. I got in and sat beside Rooney on a rear bench seat. The vehicle was filled with blue smoke.

"Where have you been?" Rooney asked with a tone fathers use to scold teenagers who return after curfew.

"Figuring things out."

"Did you get many answers?"

"Some."

"Care to explain?"

"Ask a question and I'll see what I can do."

Rooney's face brightened with the hot blood of rage as he growled, "Why were you hanging out near one of our safe houses? What do you want?"

I said, "Driver, take the GW, we're going south."

Rooney's eyebrows rose. I could actually hear his teeth grinding. A long minute ticked by before Rooney finally said, "Okay."

The agent driving nodded, accelerated.

"How far are we going, Sidney?"

"To Washington. To the NSA's HQ."

"*Ugh*. We'll take the jet. Punch it for Newark International."

As the small jet taxied and took off I smiled with the recollection that the NSA was once jokingly referred to as "No Such Agency." But the government had long since given up denying its existence.

The NSA's headquarters are located in Fort George G. Meade, Maryland, about ten miles northeast of Washington, DC. The NSA has given up on its denial of existence so much that it now even has its own exit on the Baltimore-Washington Parkway labeled "NSA Employees Only."

Rooney gave up asking questions and passed the forty-minute flight by cursing into a cell phone to a long series of people I couldn't keep track of. The plane landed at Reagan National Airport and we were soon in a Town Car zooming north on the George Washington Memorial Parkway past the Pentagon and into suburban Maryland.

A few minutes later we took an exit off Maryland Route 295 and into the NSA's headquarters. We had to wait ten minutes at a vehicle checkpoint before we were buzzed in. We drove into parking lots that can hold 18,000 autos and parked in a special lot designated for Washington brass visits next to a high-rise with glass designed to stop electromagnetic transmissions so someone couldn't use hardware, such as TEMPEST, to pick up electromagnetic radiation and thereby eavesdrop on the NSA.

The NSA had grown into the largest online security agency in the world. That it even has the ability to file for U.S. patents is under a gag order; unlike normal patents, these are not revealed to the public and do not expire; however, if the Patent Office receives an application for an identical patent from a third party, they're supposed to reveal the NSA's patent and officially grant it to the NSA for the full term on that date. For example, one of the NSA's published patents describes a method of geographically finding an individual computer. It's based on the time it takes a packet to move across a computer connection on multiple networks. This patent was only activated after a security agency developed what they thought was new technology and tried to patent it. No one knows how many more patents the NSA has.

Because of the NSA's clout, of its stranglehold on emerging technology, I'd always dreamed of going behind the NSA's firewall. I'd thought about working for the government, as every gifted computer forensics expert, code writer, and hacker does, but the bureaucracy was a turnoff. I liked being my own master, going undercover and playing various roles. I didn't like the idea of reporting to some bureaucratically appointed dunce and sitting in air-conditioning in front of glowing monitors my entire life while being used by lesser intellects for causes I may or may not agree with.

I thought the loss of my mother had made me independent. She passed away when I was twelve. My father, who was always away on business in my youth, then abandoned me, as he, for all practical purposes, abandoned reality. I finished high school while living on friends' couches. My father chose the bottle, while I found solace in computers, in the alternate reality of the digital world. It was a place I could understand, even control. I considered programming, physics, and calculus to be simple challenges I had to master to gain stability in a human world, a place where important people didn't die. Math scores placed me in the top percentile. I won a full scholarship to MIT. At first I found security in the predictable rhythm of classes, of rewards for simply getting As on tests. But I soon became bored. I found I knew more than my professors in this developing field. In my second semester I busted a hacker who had embedded a Trojan horse into MIT's financial services department. The hacker was another MIT student who decided he'd rather not pay tuition. He'd have gotten away with it too, but he became greedy and started siphoning funds from MIT accounts and putting the funds through a Cayman Islands money-laundering scheme. I took him down and felt like a superhero. No one knew how I'd traced the hacker. I tried to explain how I implanted packets for the hacker to steal that would then later ping back data on routers used and data emailed, but no one knew what I was talking about.

Jobs soon came my way as companies called MIT looking for people to protect them from the new cyber threats they little understood. The university sent the people my way. The money was easy. The work was intriguing. Before I knew it I'd dropped out of school and was making all I asked for by hunting down cybercriminals, insider traders, those involved in corporate espionage.

My father learned of my affluence and began butting into my life whenever his wallet went empty. I pitied the old man. I saw my father's alcoholism as a sign that he really did love my mother. I helped him as much as I could.

As I thought about all this, I frowned with the realization I'd forgotten all about my father. He called from a precinct . . . oh, nothing to be done now . . . he's getting what he deserves, I suppose . . . I'm so damn helpless now I can't even bail him out this time . . .

"Sidney," said Rooney, "are you listening? We're at the NSA. Now what's this all about?"

I looked up. "Right, let's go in. I want to meet the team who's hunting Verity."

"Why?"

"Technical stuff."

Rooney began muttering "Fucking generation of smart-asses" as he pulled himself out of the car and led the way into a waiting area. A guard glowered at us as Rooney said, "We're here to see Rex Baker. Tell him Rooney is here with a Truth Seeker to see him."

Ten minutes later a frail boy with the complexion of an inmate pulled from a long stay in solitary confinement stepped out, blinked in the bright light of the waiting area, and grinned at me.

"Oh, hi Feckless," said Rooney.

The pale boy ignored Rooney's provocation as he held out a pallid hand for me to shake.

I shook the cold, soft thing.

"I'm a huge fan," cooed the boy, who looked like he spent all his hours basking in the cold glow of a monitor in a controlled climate. "We've, of course, all read your file."

I supposed he meant the profile Verity had made public.

"You can follow me, but you can't take any electronics with you," said the boy as he pointed a long, opaque finger at my computer bag. "We have a controlled system, you know."

I knew the building's glass all around us was specially made to stop all signals, because even the radiation from a PC can be picked up and read from hundreds of yards away and because the NSA doesn't want information emailed in or out of the controlled portions of its network. I knew theirs is the safest network in the world. It's un-hackable because its core doesn't talk to the outside, either through fiber optics, cell towers, or satellites.

"I have something here to share with you." I handed the boy the laptop and said, "It's in your control."

The boy hesitated.

"Well, Feckless, what's it gonna be?" Rooney said.

The boy walked back to the desk, had a whispering conversation with someone on a phone, then came back, nodded, and said, "This way."

We passed through layers of security. A metal detector, an eye scanner, a bomb sniffer, a body scanner searching for hidden circuits, electronics that could be used to steal intelligence, and more and then we wended through halls of offices. As we drew deeper into the heart of the NSA, my knees grew weak. I wondered what I should do. Should I warn them? Should I tell them what I'd been asked to do? If I did, they'd react, maybe make a mistake that would cost me. Then I'd be useless to them, as Verity would certainly take his pound of flesh and toss me from his movement and into limbo. Telling them would be folding in the game of life. Once I became useless even the government would drop me. I wouldn't even be able to work for the NSA, as my loyalty would seem too tainted for the military brass running the agency to stomach. If I told them, I'd inevitably have to wander off and become a nonperson going job to job, but never becoming myself, the person I'd fought to become. But then, following Verity's orders was almost treason, so did the government deserve this action? They weren't being completely honest with me. Do I owe these people blind loyalty? Isn't America built on the idea that we don't do that with government? I thought so. I could justify and reason that Rooney told me to join Verity so they could follow me to him, but that was rationalizing.

We stopped in a glass office surrounded by cubicles filled with people in suits. A tall, lean man with a receding hairline loosened a tie worn only because he had to. He had a face the sun hadn't exposed in a decade. He grinned coffee-stained teeth at me and said, "It's a pleasure, Sidney. I'm Rex Baker. I lead the team hunting Verity."

Feckless put my computer bag on the desk and Rex looked at it as if it was slathered in feces. "So what's this about? Why have you insisted on bringing a dirty laptop in here?"

Rooney said, "That's what I've been waiting to hear."

Rex blushed and looked at Rooney. "Oh, hi Mr. Rooney. Good to see you again in person. It's been a wild year."

Rooney brushed off the friendly banter and fell into a seat.

I casually sat down, crossed my legs, and said in a flat voice, "Sit down, Rex. I'm here to talk to you."

Rex thumped nervously into a swivel chair and Feckless quietly shut the office door as he left. Neither liked how in control I seemed. They wondered just what I knew, what I was up to, if they could trust me.

This was all so very unusual. They were typically the ones with the answers, with the dirt. The NSA stayed ahead of all other governments and hackers by hiring the best and by classifying information-sharing technology when it became too advanced.

The mission statement on the NSA's public website even boasts as much: "Our Vision: Global Cryptologic Dominance through National Network Advantage. The Information Assurance mission confronts the formidable challenge of preventing foreign adversaries from gaining access to sensitive or classified national security information. The Signals Intelligence mission collects, processes, and disseminates intelligence information from foreign signals for intelligence and counterintelligence purposes and to support military operations. This Agency also enables Network Warfare operations to defeat terrorists and their organizations at home and abroad, consistent with U.S. laws and the protection of privacy and civil liberties." Of course, declarations, in the end, always turn out to be nothing more than intentions—such was their greatest dread.

"Okay, shoot," said Rex.

I hesitated, then followed the script I'd been sent: "Verity asked me to come here to see you. He asked me to tell you," I drew a deep breath, hesitated a moment more, then yelled, "KILL BIG BROTHER!"

Rooney and Rex fell back in their chairs as the words ricocheted off glass walls. Had I joined the Truth Seekers, really sided with them? They stared at me, unsure whether to call security or to laugh.

Did I just voice-activate the laptop? Was it then silently turning on and delivering whatever package Verity wanted impregnated in the heart of the NSA's system?

I waited for alarms to blare. I was poised for a signal broadcast from the laptop to be detected. They must be monitoring signals. This is the security leader in code breaking and digital intelligence. The NSA's staff was bigger than the CIA's, the FBI's, and NASA's combined. They wouldn't overlook such a basic security protocol.

Both Rooney and Rex were still staring at me. I didn't hear any alarms. No one was running in.

I finally filled the uncomfortable pause with the words, "Verity told me to say that loudly. Verity asked me to tell you to commit seppuku or he's going to blind you."

I smiled like it was all a very big joke.

"Huh?"

"Verity holds gatherings with all of the Truth Seekers. He instructs them via some encrypted code that he said you can't break. It's startling, only his eyes appear on the screen . . ." I kept speaking dramatically and the tension passed away and they began to laugh.

I relaxed, wondered if this was just another ironic sign highlighting the government's bureaucratic inefficiency.

"That's why I wanted to bring this laptop in. It must have things on it you can use, maybe even trace. I know you have the best hackers and code breakers in the world here. Verity uses the cameras on these computers to watch and judge his followers, so he must have code on there that can help you. But I have to leave here with that computer, because if I don't he'll know I've given it to you."

Rex nodded. "We can copy all the files and give it back to you. But you know we've gotten their laptops before. They've taught us things but . . . well, not enough."

Rex smiled, tilted his head as he said, "You know, Sidney, it's funny, you're not exactly what I expected."

"Oh, how so?"

"Well, I've read your whole profile. Even before Verity published all the facets of your remarkable life, I knew of you. We've wanted to recruit you for some time."

"Yes, I know, I've turned down a few offers."

"When you exposed the Chinese for hacking the New York Stock Exchange, we were impressed, though the State Department was miffed over the repercussions," said Rex. "But when you not only prevented an invasion of Pfizer by the Malaysians, but also sent them a worm that tracked down and ate all the data they stole, well, we were overwhelmed. We've learned a lot from you."

"I know. You've even classified a few of my worms."

"We do what we must. But, you know, you're not what I was expecting. I know what toilet paper you buy, that you dropped out of MIT after telling Professor Taylor 'I can stay here and be deep in debt for playing with your outdated schoolbooks, or I can leave and be rich.' I've seen photos and video of you from your high school graduation to surveillance photos we took of you last month when you nabbed a Russian mole on NASDAQ, but from your profile I thought you were a geek, uh, a social boob. But I see you're . . . well, I'm surprised. You're more debonair than I expected, more confident; you're not a boy at all."

Rex's up-front candor was refreshing. Rooney growled, "All right enough professional compliments, let's get down to business."

"Oh, poor Rooney," said Rex. "You see, Sidney, Verity sent his profile to everyone in government service months ago. It has cost him a lot of—"

"Enough!" said Rooney as he recalled why he hated these NSA geeks.

"And he's profiled me, of course," said Rex, who was turning out to be very affable. "But I'm so boring, so it didn't matter much. The thing is, a lot of personnel don't want to work on this case because they don't want the embarrassment of everything they've said or done going public. Only the really boring louts with nothing to hide are okay with hunting Verity. Which, ironically, is the way Verity says he likes it."

"*Says* he like it?"

"Oh yes, we've had many conversations with him. He's a gentleman, always stating his intentions and giving us a fair chance to change our policies before he punishes us."

"Rex," Rooney said, "let me remind you that Sidney does not have a security clearance of any kind."

"Oh yes, sorry. I talk so infrequently to field personnel, I guess I forget, and I really am a fan of yours, Sidney."

And so I spent the day talking about code and antiviral software and cutting-edge intrusion-detection techniques with the world's leading infiltrators and online spooks and mathematicians who write ingenious things the NSA can and does file patents for that no one can see, at least no one without the proper clearances.

Meanwhile, the NSA copied the laptop's contents and quietly loaded it with their eyes and ears, just as Verity said they would.

When the day was done I left NSA's HQ thinking I just might have the digital tracks to sniff a way out of this double-agent dilemma. I was playing this down the middle and trying not to be crushed between this rock and a hard place.

12

WHO IS RIGHT?

AS AMTRAK'S ACELA train carried me up the Jersey coast to New York City that Friday night I had the rudiments of a plan shaping. Before I could act, I had a question to answer: Was Verity right? As the train zoomed up a dark coast I felt bipolar, or schizophrenic, or something. I was weighing two opposite views at once while trying to find the right in both. I recalled that George Orwell defined the acceptance of two contradictory ideas or beliefs at the same time as "doublethink."

I knew I couldn't accept both answers. But which was right, or which was more right? Both Big Brother and Verity seemed partially right and partially wrong and I didn't know what to think. Was Verity right? Should all information on public officials be made public? Or was Big Brother right? Should all information be only in the hands of the state, as is increasingly occurring today?

Ground wasn't solid under my feet. Anxiety from uncharacteristic indecision sent stomach acid to my mouth as I leaned back in my seat and looked blankly out the train's window and into the autumn night. I had to decide. But how could I? The day's treason, if that is what it was, was a catalyst forcing me to finally choose sides, to come to a philosophical decision of what is right.

But had I already chosen Verity's side? I'd just done something for Verity. I'd gotten copies of the NSA's latest spyware. They, as Verity said they would, loaded it into my PC. I couldn't let myself get away with doublethink.

But if I'd really chosen sides, then why did I have to justify, to talk myself into this? And why was my stomach, my barometer, in upheaval? I'd always felt easier after a decision was made. Not this time. Something inside me knew I hadn't picked sides, not really, or perhaps that I'd chosen the wrong side, or that neither side was right . . . ?

I worried about all that and more and then thought about what Rex said. What did he mean? He'd read all about me but still didn't know me?

This admission from Rex seemed to say something important about Verity's truth, but I was too tired to think clearly, to comprehend rationally, so I let my mind succumb to my heart and Aster floated in and carried my consciousness away and I wondered if I was falling for her or just for the image of her, for what I hoped she was. I wondered if that really was what love is, our wish that someone be the perfection of all we lack, or want them to be.

I next thought that naïve, as a person hunting perfection would keep hunting for eternity; it was too superficial, too sure to lead to divorce as the flesh ages, looks wilt like dying flowers.

No, I decided, maybe love is finding, seeing, something in someone under all the human mistakes and shortfalls and loving them for keeping that one thing pure, perfect, maybe just for you. Maybe validating that love is simply offering them the same pure something. Maybe that's what we mean by true love? Something deeper, something we can only sense, a connection to another soul? In that way you both help each other be better individuals, truer to something unchanging, something divine. I shook my head. I was really too tired for such metaphysical inquiries into my confused heart. Math I understood, but this . . . ?

The train stopped at Penn Station and I walked past closed shops and down Manhattan's midnight avenues. Streetlight shimmered out of black rain puddles. I went to my hotel. I rode the elevator up to my room. I went down a hall hearing televisions and people laughing.

I went into my room and closed and locked the door. As instructed, I placed the laptop on the small desk, plugged it in, and opened it. The PC popped on and its glass eye began babysitting me, or at least that's how it felt.

I was exhausted. I stretched out along the bed and clicked on the TV. I needed to unwind, to let my mind loosen. One of those live news debate shows where the winner is the pundit who screams the loudest or makes up the most outlandish statistic popped on.

That worm of a host, Oliver Wissel, as usual had a conservative on his right and a liberal on his left, same old—but then I heard the discussion topic and dropped the remote.

Wissel, a featureless, well-proportioned face, head with perfect hair, sharp, chocolate eyes, and a bright smile, began, "Tonight, America, we're going to discuss how open to public scrutiny our politicians should be. Early this morning New York's Mayor Perkins took his own life after someone emailed detailed records to journalists that proved he was an adulterer."

Wissel paused, nodded as if he'd decided something, smiled coyly and continued, "Now Perkins' love for a fresh skirt has long been rumor, but innuendo became verifiable truth thanks to the anonymous whistle-blower known as Verity. So where did all this intel come from? And should it have been released? It wasn't done via a legal wiretap. And Perkins' profile is filled with recordings and private emails."

Wissel looked left and asked, "Senator Albert Moss, my liberal friend, tell me, did Mayor Perkins get what was coming to him or did this Verity character, if indeed he or she does exist, invade his privacy immorally?"

Mouth opening and closing like a minnow sucking for air in a dirty tank, a red and blue striped bowtie, thin hair parted on the side and combed over a freckled scalp, a nose that resembled a beak, and a skeletal figure, the liberal answered, "Oh, let's show some respect on this day of tragedy, shall we?"

Wissel shrugged, said, "No, Senator, today I think we need honesty. I don't care if Perkins was a Democrat—dishonor is not a trait either party has a patent on. Forget about Perkins. Give me a generality. Is such a thing right or wrong?"

The liberal sucked a mouthful of air before saying, "Are crimes liberties? The people have a right to know, just not at the cost of personal privacy. Judges have to okay wiretaps for a reason."

Wissel smiled, turned to the conservative, asked, "Senator Bill Harris, if you knew who this whistle-blower is, would you prosecute?"

White shirt, red tie, spine permanently slouched, head like a ripe melon, body the shape and size of a couch turned upright, the conservative said, "No, no, that's a loaded question, how can I answer that? Very little is known—"

Wissel interrupted, "Now that's not true, Senator, everything is known but the identity of the whistle-blower who calls him or herself Verity."

"Yes, well, that may be so," stalled the conservative, "but I—"

"You what? Tell me, was it right or wrong?"

"If the charges are true then Mayor Perkins should have been found out for the public's own good, but in a legal manner."

"Legal," said Wissel with a smile, "so only the government, and not the press, the people, have a right to investigate?"

"Well, you can't just take justice into your own hands. He had a right to privacy," said the conservative.

"A privacy advocate, you?" asked Wissel. "In 2002 you endorsed the formation of the Information Awareness Office as a part of DARPA so that it could create an online surveillance monster called the Total Information Awareness Program. When it grew unpopular you suggested to Admiral John Poindexter (and no, I'm not making that name up, folks) that they change the program's name to 'Terrorism Information Awareness Program' so civil libertarians would shut up."

Senator Harris turned rouge for an instant before saying, "That was totally different. We thought we were going to be attacked again at any moment and had to find terrorist sleeper cells—"

"So fear drove you to err, Senator?"

"I wouldn't put it that way."

Wissel's eyebrows shot up as he said, "You're both hiding behind undefined areas in the law. But Senator Harris, weren't your private emails and financial records made public a few weeks back?"

"Yes."

"Was that right?"

"No."

"What political price did you pay?"

"I'm ahead in the polls, as you know."

"Have they caught the person who made your private info public?"

"No."

"Do they have a lead?"

"They've spent too much time concentrating on me and my staff. They thought because I came out looking good, whereas my opponent was found to be improperly using campaign funds, that my campaign must be involved."

"So," smiled Wissel, "your eyes have been opened. And, because you're clean, the outing has actually helped you. Because you're honest, you're being rewarded. If I recall, your opponent was ahead of you in the polls when this Verity character made your profile public."

"It's an ongoing investigation. I can't discuss it further."

Wissel leaned in for the kill. "But Senator Harris, wouldn't you admit that the release of your profile was for the public good? Hasn't it served justice? Wasn't it then right?"

The conservative frowned. "The outcome in this case was just, but it wasn't right. Too often these investigations are run by politically appointed peons looking to sully reputations."

"But what if the facts were released by a nonpartisan?"

"There's no such thing."

Wissel shrugged, said, "Maybe not yet." He looked at the liberal and asked, "So, Senator Moss, does a crime committed make divulging info on a politician just?"

"Yes," said the liberal, "that is the gist of the Whistle-Blower Act."

"So then," said Wissel, "all politicians would have to be investigated for that to happen. It's just that the ones who committed a crime would be the only ones who would have their info made public?"

"Yes, I think that's right. The state can certainly handle that much," said the liberal.

"That's nonsense," said the conservative. "You're going to give the government the right to judge when someone should be publicly hung? Politics will be involved. We'll have witch hunts. Spin. Remember, we're innocent until proven guilty. Only some sort of evidence should instigate an investigation. And then the courts should handle it, not the public."

"Not the public," said Wissel, "so then, where is the check on government?"

"At the polls."

"Not unless they know the truth," said Wissel, who then asked, "So, Senators, how much privacy should the public let you have?"

Neither was prepared for the change in the direction of the question. It seemed upside down somehow. Wasn't it the government that decided how much privacy was to be allowed?

Wissel asked, "Senator Moss, would you mind if everyone knew everything?"

"No, well, the state needs to know things, but the public, uh, for their own good, uh, the government needs to protect the people," said Senator Moss.

"How about you, Senator Harris, you're on the Homeland Security and Governmental Affairs Committee. For our own safety, should the government and the government alone know everything on each individual?"

Senator Harris's scalp glowed as he said, "I wouldn't trust the state with inspecting my toothbrush. This is why we passed the Privacy Act of 1974 right after Watergate. We have to find terrorists and criminals to keep the public safe and that information needs to be in the hands of the government, but that doesn't mean we should implicitly trust the state to keep records on the citizenry. The damn government should keep its nose out of our business unless damn necessary." *Gulp!* For a moment he forgot he was on public television.

Wissel flashed his perfect teeth, asked, "But Senator Harris, you are a Republican, and you voted for the Patriot Act."

"Yes, well, we did what we had to after September 11."

"And wasn't the Privacy Act of 1974 amended in 2007 following a controversial agreement with the EU that now gives the Department of Homeland Security access to individual records on millions of Americans in the Arrival and Departure

System, uh, A-D-I-S, so that law-enforcement can utilize personal data to clear passengers through a watch list?"

"Again, that was necessary considering—"

"But who is making certain the list isn't abused?"

"Well our federal agencies—"

"So the fox is watching the henhouse. Why can't the list simply be made public?"

"Well I don't, I mean, some things have to remain classified."

Wissel shook his head as he shifted to the Democrat and asked, "Didn't you also vote for the Patriot Act, Senator?"

"Well yes, but they didn't give us time to read it, but, well, I think it does certainly need to be amended as necessary—"

Wissel's eyes were gleaming as the show went to a commercial.

I turned off the television and, as I grasped for right and wrong in this new digital age, I succumbed to fatigue and fell into a sleep of living nightmares.

13

AM I THIS PROFILE?

I WOKE IN my hotel room at 3:00 a.m. Saturday morning. My mind was raging: "Rex and the others at the NSA all commented I wasn't what they'd expected. What did they mean? How could they not know me? They knew everything about me. That makes no sense. My whole life is there in my profile, isn't it?"

I sat up and looked around the tiny hotel room in the almost darkness of the city that never sleeps and the room began to spin. I shut my eyes as I thought, strange, I didn't drink, why do I have the spins?

The cause was only a head rush from transitioning from the subconscious to reality too abruptly. I stood and began to pace as I softly muttered, ever careful of the laptop overhearing, "If they don't know me, even though they've studied me, then how is anyone to know anyone if profiles are made public? This includes politicians, doesn't it? How can anyone possibly have the time anyway? It's impossible. We'll be making the same judgments we do today, only worse, the journalists will be gone, replaced by masters of spin. Sure, many are that way now, but it'll be worse. No one will work for a scoop, they'll just do some kind of Google search or whatever and then add their opinion to the menu. There wouldn't be a professional left among them. Any standards now left would be dashed."

I sat on the bed and dropped my head into my hands. I thought things had been going this way a long time, that this was inevitable. Slowly, year after year, journalism was speeding up and losing its details to anonymous sources and partisan spin and empty statistics and competing polls that were only reflections of the spin. Then I knew there wouldn't be more truth with more so-called facts from Verity, but just more intense spin, out-of-context judgments. I knew reporting was a dying art. Now so many just Google or Yahoo or something and then steal facts and repeat fallacies and add their spin while everyone in the Beltway watches polls, endless series of polls that only judge opinion, reactions to the spin, and so it goes ever faster round and round until we're all too dizzy to see, to know a damn thing.

I ran my fingers through my hair and looked up at the white ceiling in the almost dark room. I reached across the bed and flipped on a light and saw the blue binder that held my profile. It lay where I'd tossed it, solemnly in a corner.

I slowly turned my gaze to the open laptop on the desk like I'd just noticed another person in the room, a person watching me intently. I blushed. Quickly told myself to yawn. Did so. Got back in bed. Flipped off the light, let minutes pass, then slipped out of bed on the far side from the laptop and crawled along the carpet being ever so careful to keep the bed between myself and the staring laptop camera.

I snatched the blue binder that held my profile and slithered into the bathroom, out of sight of the laptop's unblinking glass eye. I quietly closed the door and turned on the small light over the sink and began to read, to really read this time, between the lines, to understand what the profile meant, was determining, would do.

I saw things differently then, with a more educated eye than I had when I'd first read the summation of my existence. I soon found meeting yourself is one thing, but reading every detail, along with thousands of comments from friends and family, authoritarians and foes, is another. I saw the results from a third-grade IQ test. Saw that Mrs. Stewart, my teacher, had scribbled in the margin, "Sidney must have cheated; he's not this bright." I read email conversations between girls I'd dated and their friends. I found over and over that they liked my looks, but found me too distant. Some thought I was elitist, others shy, but my nonconformity was always weighed against me. Many of the girls tweaked each critique with a personal pronoun; such as, "I'm too deep for him" or "he's not for me at all" or "he'd be just too difficult to change. I mean, it would be a lot of work to make him into the right kind of person for me." Their perspectives always took precedence over mine. Over and over I found myself thinking I'm not someone else's perception. I refused to define myself by their impressions, by their shallow, selfish observations and desires.

After perusing six hundred pages of critiques and comments from everyone I ever knew, after reading my own emails, college research papers, financial, medical, and criminal records, even the diary I'd always added to at my most dramatic moments—times when I needed the release—I read my synopsis, what amounted to a psych profile, and went into a rage. This thing categorized me. This damn thing determined my proper occupation as a technical police officer, someone who solved online crime. My profile said I needed a bureaucracy to help with my antisocial behavior. To be completely useful to this society, my profile determined I needed to be watched, guided, kept from my propensity to go it alone, that I needed reins to turn me in useful directions, spurs to drive me faster. I needed the NSA as a master.

Standing, shaking my fists, I cursed under my breath as a madman mutters and speaks as if he is only hearing himself from across a dark room: "Bullshit. I'm not this. This is one-dimensional. It's all out of context. The image I get of this person, this fictional bastard, is a confused, introverted, shallow, young white male with no capability for love or depth. He . . . he seems more like a machine, a computer with some ability to locate online criminals, but who has no real emotions. On paper, this person is a cartoon character. He lacks meaning between the lines. He's insensitive and judgmental. He doesn't hate or love his life; he's impartial to living. He's destined to be a reclusive user, a hermit in a big city who hides from sight in a cloak of mediocrity. None of my humor, my joy of life, my philosophy on fighting for right is here. This thing may be my surface, my reflection, but it's not me. People, places, I feel them, I smell them, I hear them, I don't just see them. On paper? Who is this guy? He's dry; he's thankless; his jokes are flat. He's outweighed by his judges, his jury; he's measured by the depth of their comments, by their thoughts and bias. This person, this profile, would I hire him? Would I want to know him? What's here is too cold, too guileless. A life on white paper isn't a life. A soul has more than two dimensions. Like a book, this profile is read through the reader's personal perspective, feelings, and emotions, not from the individual who's been profiled; you can't step into another's mind through a piece of paper or a computer screen. We can relate, we can't possess. Verity is wrong."

My whole worldview spun around. I came to the conclusion that at best people work their entire lives to be who they want, who they dream of being, while their physical bodies age and get sick and, at its purest, is but a physical representation of them.

I thought you try to make yourself into what you are, or wish to be, and along the way we'll fail and we'll succeed, but all along we need to simply try to be ourselves despite physical limitations in order to achieve all that's worthwhile. I came to the conclusion that Verity was right that some people let others define them by their appearance, instead of using their appearance to be who they are at their best, but I also concluded that Verity wasn't right about taking away free will with profiles designed to guide us, to lead us, to be our masters.

The Truth Seekers' profiles—created from test scores, genetic histories, buying tendencies, criminal records, and more—are false, because they're no more than slices of life, photos from an existence that is always flowing, always changing, never the same. Sure, you can be who you are within on the outside, in the physical world, but only if you keep who you are pure on the inside, only if you define yourself. Being pure means having privacy, as no one can really ever completely know you. This is why this profiling system eventually had to fit people into types, into subgroups, as if all of the billions of people in the world were simply just ten thousand, with some copied many times over.

As I stood in the hotel bathroom out of sight from my laptop in the darkest hour of the October night I knew in my head and heart that people need the freedom to be individuals, whether they fail or succeed, in order to attain real progress. Profiling the populace would end the progress created by individual freedom. Verity was wrong.

Verity was wrong, wrong, wrong, I knew as I clenched my fists quietly in the bathroom and didn't speak for fear the laptop would eavesdrop and pass on my contentious conclusions.

Maybe Verity's system could help a few lost souls, I thought. People could go to some center and give Verity everything and then let the program do the math. This would help some purify themselves into what was fundamental, what was most important to them, closer to their potential. But that's only psychotherapy for a few lost souls. It doesn't make profiling a populace right;

it only makes Verity a modern psychologist, not a prophet for a new, collective order.

"Damn this thing!"

I impulsively threw the blue binder into the bathtub and raged in a whisper, "Verity you're wrong! You're wrong! People shouldn't be profiled like this. I'm not this bundle of paper! Verity!"

14

THE INDIVIDUAL WAKES

ASTER WAS THERE on my laptop at 8:00 a.m. Saturday morning.

"Sidney . . . Sidney, are you still sleeping? Thought you'd like to know your mission was a success."

I rolled over, looked at her face shown through the fish-eye lens of her laptop.

"Yes, fine," I said yawning and my mind jumping.

"Let's do brunch," she said. "It's Saturday and it's a lovely autumn morning and we have another mission to discuss. Something big is coming. I'm to prepare you for some things. I think this could be it. The day of reckoning is at hand."

She sounded so excited. I looked at her closely. She was lovely, but so idealistic, so sure she was right, too sure she was right. She hadn't questioned this enough; it felt right so she went along and was sucked into this cult by its charismatic leader and now was too deep to see the surface.

Yes, I knew, deep down, no, all through myself, I disagreed with her. I wondered whether she could come around, if further thought might awaken her individual mind or if that was just my own lust weighing in, wanting her.

"Sidney, you okay?" asked Aster. "You seem to be someplace else."

"Oh, just waking up. I'll meet you in an hour at the clock in Grand Central. There are some cafés there that are quite good."

As I was speaking I was thinking: The tracks in the lower tunnels won't let GPS signals through. That could be just the place.

Aster was coming through the light Saturday morning crowd in Grand Central Station. She seemed to have a spotlight following her over the marble floor while all around her was just black-and-white background. I was falling for her.

But will she betray Verity with me, or turn me in?

She waded into a mob of children wearing masks of goblins and Disney sweethearts who were all being led by three women ushering them along the floors of Grand Central.

Ah, it's Halloween again, I realized. I smiled to myself at how I'd lost track of time, of the season. But I didn't lose track of her.

Aster passed through the group of children patting heads as she went. She was all lit up in her white overcoat tied at the waist to show off her figure topped with a snow-white smile. I hoped she was looking her best for me, but really didn't think this was her best, but was just her.

Then she was there and we were walking together seemingly to nowhere in particular, though I knew just where in particular. I led her downstairs to the lower tracks where the air would be cave-like if it weren't for the charged odor of trains using third rails. I checked my phone. Kept walking to dark recesses. Checked again. Nodded. Turned it off. Stopped. Asked, "Aster, please turn off your phone."

"Why'd we come down here? Looks like a good place for a murder," she teased nervously.

"This is no joke," I said as I looked intensely in her eyes, "I've made a decision and want to know where you stand."

"Uh, Sidney I—"

"*Shhh*, this is serious. This is everything."

She turned off her phone, said, "Okay," as she suddenly looked so serious.

"I've decided they're both wrong."

"Both?"

"Verity and the government, uh, Big Brother. They're both half right and wrong and if I . . . or we, side with either we'll be only half right and therefore so terribly wrong."

"Sidney, what are you talking about?"

"I'm going to betray Verity, but not to the government; no, to the people. I have a plan. It's a long shot."

Aster started to walk away. Stopped. Turned wet animated eyes back into me. Her eyes flashed and her mouth glimmered in the flickering fluorescent light as she said, "Sidney, Verity gave me my life. Without him the hand of Big Brother would have kept defining me all my life and everything would have been meaningless because it never would have been mine, been me, I'd have always been someone else."

I stepped forward and took her elbows gently with my hands as I looked into her glistening eyes and explained as calmly as I could, "Yes, he did, and that was right, but the rest is and will be used to define you by averages. I read my profile. I met the NSA people who'd read all about me and who'd been watching me for years and found that their conception of me was out of context. I saw that is not me in that profile, but a skewed picture of me. Aster, we can't be defined in black and white. Such profiling leads to assumptions, to others judging us by their biases, as they did you. People can't see the three-dimensional that way. They make suppositions. It's like defining a client for a jury. All the legal facts are there but the attorney still has to humanize the defendant and thereby shape the person for their dozen peers to digest, to fit into stereotypes of guilt or innocence. It's there that Verity goes wrong. Killing Big Brother by shining light on him would accomplish exactly what it's designed to end.

"Aster, racial bias will become IQ bias or something and no one will ever be able to grow and learn from a mistake because the error will always be there in black and white as if it happened yesterday. And you won't be able to escape it, to grow, to develop.

"And the government isn't right either. They're keeping files on more and more of us. They're putting us on watch lists and criminal lists and now digitizing our medical records. And they'll, sooner or later, combine and cross-reference all those records. But even then, they can't know you really. Not by your medical, criminal, educational, or other records or by what you read or bought. If this goes on, they'll make categories; they'll grow stronger as the world becomes increasingly digital; before long we'll be living in an Orwellian world if either Verity or Big Brother wins."

I took a breath and stepped back from her and saw she was crying.

"Aster, consider your own profile, not Verity's but Big Brother's, the one you fought to see. It's right that you got to see what all those government experts were saying about you, so that you could take control of your own life, but should everyone be able to see all that about you? It'd be taken out of context. You'd be judged by parts of the profile. How many would read the entire thing; and, even if they did, how many would understand you? In Verity's world, sure you get to see, to know everything, but you'll never be able to be you, not really, because everyone who matters will judge you by parts, by their own perceptions of you and you'll never be able to escape their prying eyes."

Aster wiped a tear away. Bit her lip. Sighed. "Perhaps you're right," she whispered. "I don't know."

We stood there a long moment looking at each other. Aster's expression said she was thinking back over years of working for Verity, through law school, and so much more. She, I hoped, was starting to realize she'd fallen under the spell of a cult leader. She thought she was being so independent, but now saw she was just following another path someone else had cleared for her. But she was clearly reluctant to make the same mistake again, especially when our chances of success were so slim. She didn't know if she agreed with me, if she could help me, nor did she know if she wanted to help me.

My mind was running steps ahead. I wanted to get free of these chains, to outrun whatever was happening, even if I was wrong.

"Aster," I said as I bent over slightly to find her castaway gaze, "I've been thinking, if he is able to gather so much information so quickly and easily, then he must have developed a virus. Something our scanning software doesn't see. A combination it doesn't know to look for. Like that 'I-have-pictures-of-you' virus. That code seemed normal, harmless, until it combined inside a server. What if he has so infected our networks, the whole net, with something that on its face seems normal?"

"Sidney," her voice cracked like an adolescent's.

I kept rattling away to cover my own uncertainty. "A malicious worm, pieces of code so small they don't jump out, something that hides right in the source code. Something that then links into chains or even grabs information randomly, carries it out and reforms it elsewhere by tagging along on normal packages, maybe on compressed data, through routers. It's possible then that he could simply seek information on anyone with the right sort of shopbot. Some catalyst, a code that starts another code sending in a random order, using some type of cryptography, some algorithm that could then be reassembled on the other end.

If so, he wouldn't even need a server, or at least not a very big one."

Aster began to cry, to shake.

I stopped, looked softly into her wet eyes and asked, "What do you think? It's a long shot. But if I write a worm that travels in pieces, something that he searches for, like say, something about us, so we know it'll be gathered . . . then, when it's sucked up with all of his information, it will go to the origin, the place where all this is being assembled. There it could recombine and email me the location."

"Sidney," she said, "what if his is the only real way? Maybe you should think of that first."

"Aster, he's not right. Oh, his ideology is seductive. But all I know is who I am and that profile is not me. And, you know, it may sound brainless, but my job is to protect information, not to make everything public. Catching cybercriminals is what I do. I think it's what I'm meant to do."

She lowered her chin and let her shoulders loosen, slump. Then her eyes flashed up at me as her voice objected, "But Sidney, how can you let Big Brother live?"

"Verity's way isn't the only way. Look, speaking to Verity in Grand Central was the most incredible single event in my life. I can't look in the mirror now without wondering who I am, but . . . this is who I am. I think even he can understand that. I catch cybercriminals. Besides, every melancholy moment when I think I should consider his ideology, when I decide that he is on to something, I think again of those lives he's ruined with his so-called truth. His way is not the answer, that much I know. His way is terror and out-of-context judgment; it would be like living in a small town where everyone knows everyone's business and never being able to outgrow some foolish or mixed-up mistakes from so long ago."

Aster wilted like a flower out of water. Her eyes were opening wider than ever before and seeing a dark world with no hope, no hope at all for happiness.

We turned on our phones and strolled without a destination as we talked for hours. We left the tunnels and went along streets busying as shops opened. We stepped over steaming manhole covers and passed street vendors who were pushing burned coffee and stale donuts on passersby. All the while our conversation grew serious and personal and neither of us held back anything. We were connecting in the same moment, the same turmoil, and found in each other something we always knew was in us.

Aster put her arms around my neck and drew close as people pushed past on a sidewalk and she whispered, "You're right. I've known it for a long time, but wouldn't let myself think about, understand it. I'm with you, you're right, even though I think we're going to lose, that we can't possibly win, that this will get us jailed, maybe killed."

I hugged her and smelled her perfume deeply as I said, "Yes, it's a long, long shot."

Aster peeked over my shoulder at her watch and gasped and said we needed to go. We knew our cursory plan would probably get us killed or locked up or, at the very least, profiled and therefore banished from our dreams forever. Still, it was the only chance we had to come out of this as free individuals. And I wouldn't have it any other way. And with her newly opened eyes, Aster wouldn't either.

We'd make our move at the gathering at midnight.

15

WAR

I FOLLOWED ASTER out of the crisp autumn air and into her building feeling like I was entering a convenience store with a shotgun.

Her flat on Madison Avenue just a block from Central Park was just four hundred square feet and filled with the smart books of a hardworking attorney and small, elegant pieces of furniture. I noticed these things as pieces of her but mostly found her aroma in this fashionable, little apartment intoxicating, an aroma as sweet as the flower she'd chosen to be named after. But I knew our decision to fight on our own terms made this move both brave and dire, that this place was both alluring and explosive. So instead of the sweet lullaby that being allowed into her private domain should have been, I felt like a Doughboy about to leap over the parapet.

I heard but didn't listen to traffic honking along a dozen floors below as if it was the background noise of a river. She went into a cubbyhole of a kitchen to brew tea. I looked across the room at her computer and grew very serious.

I stalked across the apartment, disconnected the computer from the internet, then took a deep breath.

"We're disconnected," I said as she came in frowning.

"He'll know. He may even call," she said.

"We'll just say the modem is bad. That it'll be fixed soon."

"He'll never believe that. He always knows the truth. Sometimes I think he can read minds," she said.

"Yeah, I know all about the software he's using. But don't worry, he'll want to see us, to read our thoughts through our expressions, our eyes. That's when we'll get him."

"Can you really do all that?"

"I've done this many times before. When I think I have a hacker on the inside pegged, but can't be sure by his or her online movements, I sometimes use their PC's camera to watch them. I also use a keylogging program to read their keystrokes. The videos are always helpful in court. Juries love them. We need faces to humanize things before we can really cast judgment."

Aster was shaking her head. "Verity puts his scary eyes on the screen and watches, but I wonder sometimes what would happen if we could watch him right back. I don't think he wants the judgment he dishes out."

I sat on a small desk chair. "Yeah, I remember him saying he wants us to judge him by him, not by his appearance. I agree, he probably couldn't take it himself, which is why we're going to try and see him."

Aster looked down at the hardwood floor and crossed her arms over her stomach, then flashed her lovely eyes up at me as she said, "A man afraid of his own reflection. I wonder if he even looks at himself in the mirror. I doubt it you know. He's even afraid of *his* own judgment of himself. He's a very sick man, isn't he?"

"Yes, there's a reason the Catholic Church doesn't canonize a saint until long after their death. They have to wait until the person becomes a two-dimensional conception, until they lose the physical bias of first-person memories. Yes, I think Verity is trying to do that to himself."

Aster shifted her gaze back to the computer. "Sidney, you really used to watch people too?"

I felt my face blush. "Well, it's not spying when they're at work, on another man's dime. Court decisions have consistently found employees have no right to privacy from their employers while they're at the workplace."

"Now you're justifying."

"Maybe, but all online surveillance isn't wrong. There are just and moral rules to everything. It's just that technology has outpaced our understanding of online morality. I think that's why we're so confused. It's hard to know what's right and wrong with this stuff."

I stopped a moment before starting again: "It can be done. I've written programs to watch people quietly. It all depends on which software Verity is using to watch us, to show us his eyes. It all depends on how smart whoever set up his system really is. But, you know, I've never met anyone I couldn't beat at this game."

"You're one of those geeky kids who understand this stuff, huh?"

"Yeah, one of those guys you wouldn't have looked twice at in high school. But you know, I feel like a script kiddie just now, one of those crackers who use code they don't even understand. You see, I'll have to use a lot of code others have written to pull this off. I'll just have to get into some source code and write a few patches so they can . . ." My voice trailed off as I went into cyberspace.

I was like that for hours, typing, preparing, coding, moving software from my computer to her laptop, then Aster said, "Sidney, it's almost midnight."

My body stiffened as I asked, "Are you ready? You need to get your game face on. Remember, don't give anything away."

"I know," she said and took a seat beside me as if we were about to face a judge and jury together to hear our sentence.

I let the PC's camera pop on and the computer talk freely to the network.

Eyes immediately flashed onto the screen. Brown living eyes, a glare probing back and forth at both of us equally. Then a computer-altered voice accused, "Where have you two been? You know the rules."

Aster began to tell the prepared lie but I pinched her and said, "The truth is, uh, we wanted a little privacy . . . you see," I tossed my eyes back at the bed, then back to Verity as I blushed.

"You're young, aren't you," Verity asked rhetorically.

Aster blushed at the implication, giving the ruse believability.

"Very well, I understand, just stay connected from now on; it has become critical."

Verity's glare went elsewhere as he began preaching. "All my children you are now with me and with me in the truth. All the truth and nothing but the truth will be known, will be lived, here and now. The day we've been awaiting, we've been working for, is almost upon us, my children of the true word. The truth needs you now more than ever."

As Verity spoke I was typing, programming madly. I needed to follow the stream of zeros and ones flowing from somewhere to watch him; I needed to get it to accept a reverse connection, for it to open a packet and give me some conversation. Aster's computer was recording, was saving the images appearing on the screen to the hard drive and to several destinations in the cloud. All I needed was a glimpse, something, anything to work with.

Aster and I kept our faces as still as people posing for a picture for a long time as Verity spoke. We repeated "your word is true" at the proper moments even as I kept programming, hacking.

Then suddenly I was conversing with Verity's computer. I'd found a way in, a path, a connection through a port. I began typing faster, writing code, sending programming all the while remaining stoic, all the while hoping not to be caught before I could glimpse the master.

The computer language was a composite, but I recognized it. The basic software was one I'd worked with many times. Network intrusion was my expertise . . . then pop, a living image flashed on the screen of a man as hairless as a chemo patient but was gone so fast we barely had time to focus on its weak chin, narrow brow, small ears.

We couldn't hide our surprise; we both jumped at the screen and then it was gone and Verity's eyes were on us.

A pause, then Verity began to seethe. "Traitors. We have traitors. My Truth Seekers, we have traitors in our midst. Two Judas's are among us. They are Sidney McDaniel and Nancy Coldworth. You will meet true judgment now," said Verity before saying, "may God have mercy on your souls."

Verity's eyes vanished. I pulled out the network connection and closed the laptop. I began repeating, "Did you see him? Did you recognize him?"

"I don't know," said Aster.

"He looked familiar," I said.

"Like a chameleon," Aster thought aloud.

"That bald head, that nose, that chin . . . have I seen them before?"

Then Aster's eyebrows shot up with her voice. "We have to run." She was suddenly so aware of our dilemma. "He'll send them here. Right away. The FBI or worse. We haven't a chance. We have to run. Now!"

I stuffed our laptops in my computer bag and we grabbed our coats and dashed for the door and the stairs and then through the midnight streets.

16

RETREAT

WE RAN SIX blocks before slowing, skulking into a subway tunnel. As our chests heaved in cold night air we went down into the living cellar of the city. We watched for tails slipping through the underground lights. No one was coming. We took a train east, then south. As the subway rattled through tunnels and the fluorescents flickered Aster drew close to me. I pulled her all the way in and we kissed as naturally as if we'd done it so many times before.

Desire crackled our nerves, intoxicated us with lust, sparked deep-down yearning so real it was almost visible in some spectrum only true lovers see in their most staggering moments. The electric feeling reddened our lips. I'd never felt this way before. Overwhelmed. As adrenaline subsided to relief love fused us like champagne happiness and our bodies pressed together as if we were one.

We leaned into each other in a corner of a subway car as tunnel lights flashed through the car and over us making us look like frames moving slowly through an old-fashioned movie camera. An old woman in a mothballed dress and a young man in a hip-hop costume stared at us as the subway clanked over rails and the light flashed over Aster and me. We were too intoxicating not to stare at. I slowly rubbed my cheek against the soft skin of her cheek sending sparks cascading over and through us. Our arms tied each other together as those in love do at times of great passion or parting.

The train clanked and rattled to a stop at 33rd and Park. I smelled nectar in Aster's strawberry hair as I looked up and out the grimy windows to the platform and saw Special Agent Bent coming, tracking us with something in his palm. Bent had the look of a cat creeping toward prey. This man had reason to personally hate Verity. This man was twisted with angst for revenge.

I spun Aster around and she knew, by the desperation in my eyes we were being hunted. And worse, that the predator was close. We ran car to car. Bent saw the haste of our motion. He charged.

Bent was gaining. He had a handgun. I pushed shoulder first through a group of partiers on their way back from pubs, through a late-night crowd all holding poles and bars to steady their intentionally unsteadied feet on the rocking subway.

The sound warning the doors were closing was blaring and I didn't hear it as much as felt the sound as one does a panicked pulse.

I lurched at the sliding doors as the subway doors slid shut. Aster had my right hand; my left hand and chest pushed the doors open. Just as they opened I jumped forward to the platform, pulling her behind. But in the middle of my leap her hand was ripped from mine.

I fell hard on cold cement. My laptop slapped me on the side. I looked up and back and saw the doors close as Special Agent Bent put his long, hairy arms around Aster. I wanted to kill Bent then. The goon was holding my girl as a lover does, as I had a moment before. But then the train was going and gone and I saw her flash away in the loving embrace of Big Brother.

"The fucking phone," I cursed, realizing we'd turned on our phones to placate Verity, and then, in the rush to run, hadn't turned them off again. I knew Verity must have sent our GPS tracking info to Rooney's team. We'd made a stupid, amateur mistake and now Aster was nabbed and who knows what.

I rolled to my feet. I sprinted away as I turned off my phone and pulled its battery out. Police would be coming. I had no time, no time at all. My eyes were blurry, wet, dripping. My heart was pounding. My hands felt numb, tingly. My stomach was heaving. Stomach acid filled my mouth. I gulped my stomach's contents back down as I ran.

I couldn't let myself fall apart. I needed to get away. I knew I could only bargain for her release from a position of power.

I went up onto the street and strode up Park Avenue before cutting west to Madison Avenue and then farther west to where I didn't know.

As my passion cooled I recalled a television program on a bounty hunter who'd said the young are the hardest to track down because they're the most difficult to profile, as they don't even know what they want to do or where they want to go. I thought I'd be better off not thinking too much just now. I needed to be difficult to profile. There was no telling what Verity's profile of me might give the FBI.

I needed to melt into society, to play someone else, at least until I could formulate a plan of attack. I'd been so stupid. I began to think running wasn't even a palatable option; not when they'd taken the first girl I'd ever really fallen for. Yes, I conceded, I'd become a cornered animal; I had to fight with teeth, claws, and all my will, even if the odds were horrifying.

17

LYING WITH THE DEAD

WELL AFTER MIDNIGHT I meandered along dark
Manhattan streets as gusts of a November warm front blew
shopping bags, fast-food wrappers down alleys, over avenues. I
was talking to myself as a madman does: "You fucking idiot. You
idiot. Do you know what you've done? You dumb, stupid . . ."

People jaywalked to avoid me. I began to clench and unclench
my fists, to stomp my feet as I cursed myself to damnation.
Then my left arm struck the computer bag that was still strapped
habitually around me. I stopped, caressed the bag thinking of
the computers inside. They might have the weapons installed I
needed. The villain's face, Verity's damned image, was in there,
saved and ready to be exploited. But how?

An idea brought calm. I had a direction, a path. I didn't know
how far I'd make it, but I at least had something, a clue to use in
the hunt. Sure I was homeless, a fugitive, a piece of detritus cast
away by a society of profiled people running back and forth along
electronic leashes, but I had a direction that led over obstacles and
potentially to victory. In the path of life, I learned that is really all
someone needs, just that guiding light of individual hope. Verity
could be my bargaining chip for Aster. But how?

As I walked I considered the dilemma. My accounts would be watched again, likely refrozen. Using a credit card or attempting to withdraw cash would draw the police just as fast as they could come. I wouldn't worry about money yet. Didn't need to. I could live and purchase what I needed because I had prepared for such an event. And anyway, if I failed, it would be too soon for my lack of money to matter; if I failed I'd be dead or a ward of the state within days, which, to me, was dying prolonged, nothing more.

I thought of Verity's system. To hack the system I'd have to work through filters, zombie computers that would strip out my IP address. I'd have to be ready for cyberwar. There was a lot of preparing to do. I needed tools, online weaponry.

I tried to visualize Verity's face. I'd only seen it for a moment. What I saw was *completely* hairless, purposely bald, a bare canvas for whatever character Verity wanted to manufacture. But somehow he seemed familiar. Verity was an old white guy. He had brown piercing eyes and very proportional good looks that had aged gray, bloodless. He was a person who could be almost anyone he chose to be. As he would say, he was lucky.

I'd have to find a quiet place to sit, somewhere I could turn on these laptops and view the recording again of Verity's face. I thought maybe I could use facial-recognition software to identify him, even though I conceded it was unlikely to lead to him. Facial-recognition software was very beatable. All you had to do was use a costume, even just glasses and other small alterations could throw off the mathematical proportions a computer needs to calculate a number. Verity, who was a master of disguise, would certainly be savvy enough to keep the NSA at bay by changing his facial proportions whenever he appeared in public.

I then realized why Verity seemed to like me; why he'd taken the time to personally show me the system. We had a lot in common. We both were morphing ourselves to be who we wanted to be by wearing disguises. Now sure, everyone wears disguises, it's just that most don't acknowledge it. Everyone dresses to fit their parts. People wear uniforms as cops and fireman, nurses and hostesses, businesspeople and beauticians, but we also layer ourselves in outfits that fit us into cliques like hikers and bikers and baseball fans and intellectuals and even, ironically, nonconformists. Every time people get dressed they put on a disguise. Many even play many parts in any given day or week with disguises, costumes that even those who know us might not recognize us in. Verity knew this. He used the facades to find safety in anonymity, because you can only really be yourself when you're not allowing yourself to be defined by your judges.

Such was why Verity saw me as a prodigy; we were both online gurus, hackers, and coders well ahead of our peers. Only, of course, we had a fundamental difference: we both thought we were right, though one wanted to kill Big Brother by outing everything, the other wanted to starve Big Brother by hiding as much as possible from him.

To win this battle of worldviews, I'd have to hack Verity's profiling system, and I'd have to do it soon, as the day of reckoning was coming.

The image of Verity recorded in the laptop gave me something; I could always use this video to bargain with the FBI for my freedom and for Aster's, though I knew it wouldn't be enough. I needed more. I wasn't even sure if helping the government would be good for the public. The government would want to suppress what Verity had been up to by classifying his techniques. I wondered, if this case was kept from the public, then how could I ever really get my freedom back? I was a wanted man. Even if the charges were all dropped I'd still be tainted. And besides, if they caught Verity, they'd use his virus or whatever he had to spy on and watch the American people.

As I walked and schemed in the glare of streetlights I found myself in Times Square again and looked up at a huge screen. I saw a commercial for a presidential debate Sunday night: the faces of the two candidates smashed into each other, exploded, and then the headline "Political Fight Night at the Garden" appeared.

I kept walking, thinking. Could that be it? It would make sense. Why not profile them both on Election Day, or before, maybe during the debate.

I shook my head—maybe, maybe not. I needed more answers before I could find a way through this. I was a wanted man. Aster was in custody and I didn't know what they'd charge her with. She must be under intense questioning. I shook my head to toss the worry.

Though weary with fatigue, I fixated on the notion that the only way to get to Verity and the feds would be to hack into Verity's profiling system and take control of or copy the virus or whatever was there, anything to barter with for Aster, for myself.

I felt so selfish as I recalled that my no-good father had been exposed by Verity and arrested for insider trading or something. Could I help him too? Should I? I wasn't sure. Justice still means something, doesn't it?

I waved at a passing taxi. I got in the cab, heard the screeching tunes of Bollywood, and said before I'd even thought what to say, "The Green-Wood Cemetery, Brooklyn."

"At this hour?"

"Just go."

I had to climb over an iron fence but knew just where to go in the 478-acre cemetery to find the little stone that was my mother's. I stopped above her grave in moonless darkness and sat against a towering sepulcher that had an angel on its top that looked more like a gargoyle in the overcast November night.

I opened Aster's laptop and fired it up. The warm glow from the screen made me feel at home. I opened the file with Verity's fleeting picture and stopped the frame. There he was, a thin, white, hairless man with average features. I leaned close to the screen and smiled when I realized Verity didn't even have eyebrows. This was his clean canvas. From here he'd create his characters. No, I couldn't recognize him from this, but it was a beginning. I shut off the laptop to save the battery and leaned back on cold, hard stone.

While considering this dilemma, I fell asleep with the dead and passed the darkest hours with them.

I woke with cold as deep as poison in my sinew Sunday morning. I sat up shivering violently under a cloudless lavender sky. I marveled at the grandeur of nature, loved that it continued despite my plight. Forgot the shivers as the sun climbed and the Earth sparked scarlet light all backlit on the banks of mist that caught fire and burned over Brooklyn.

I looked over the cold marble of perhaps the most pretentious section in the graveyard and read the name on the stone with the angel: "Alfred Worthington 1852–1931." Under his name was the declaration, "Here lies a man of great importance."

"Yeah, so important he had to declare it over his own rotting corpse," I said, picturing Alfred as a pretentious turn of the century factory owner who paid immigrants pennies a day to make shoes.

I noticed down below, at the base of the hill, were little headstones that marked where Alfred's toilers lay, and I cynically conceded that even in death they were rotting under his feet.

I saw a small stone on my left, hidden in the grass: "Gerty Williams 1916–1979." And the word "Faithful." I pictured a tough woman who raised eight kids to work and die on Normandy's beaches. I looked at other stones and thought about them and who they might have been. I realized, like Verity's profiles, I couldn't know anything from words on stones any better than letters on screens. Even video was unrevealing, as it led you to judge too much by appearance and too little by the person under the attire and physique.

I gritted my teeth and knew people shouldn't be judged this way. We should struggle to know and respect each other, but shouldn't profile and categorize each other for our own benefit or peace of mind. Unless someone harms someone else's liberty, they should be free to be themselves without these judgments. I thought that we shouldn't be profiled by Big Brother or Verity or anyone unless we commit some injustice that then must be paid for. And after it's paid for, we should be left alone again.

I knew sexual offenders were an exception, and that when you have one exception, well . . . the door is open to Big Brother to step in and make us all feel safer by taking away our liberty, one feel-good piece at a time.

All that sounded complicated and unfathomable as my mind dove into the roots of a republic based on individual liberty, but I thought freedom wasn't really so convoluted. Individual rights are what gave the multitudes who came to the United States the ability to create material wealth via individual expression and their quest for a better life. There is even a phrase coined to capture this republic's individual freedom to fail or to succeed: "the American dream." Such was the basis of why I thought Verity had to be as wrong as Big Brother. Yes, I was certain, this was the fight of my life; maybe even what I'd been preparing for all these years.

I walked down the hill as the sun rose behind me projecting early orange light over leafless trees and sat in dead grass wet from dew by my mother's grave. The day would be sultry for November. The sun felt grand as warming rays fermented a positive outlook. I read her name. "Holly McDaniel September

1, 1960–October 25, 2000." There was nothing else. I always hated that there was nothing else. Now I raged at my father for only purchasing her this little meaningless stone. She was so much more. She glowed with compassion. She was a warm presence that was always constant. She never took her love away or was petty or weak. She'd always tell you what was right, and would do what was right. She was our guiding light. Her death extinguished the gayety in me and my father and nothing had been the same ever since. Yes, I knew, you can't put a person in words, not really, and especially not on a stone. Even the best novels struggle to bring a person to life with blood in their veins and angst in their hearts.

She had been the warmth for us. Since her death we'd been wandering a cold wood with other walking dead looking for something we couldn't find, because we didn't know how to find what they were looking for. I decided to some day, if I ever find myself free with all this done, to add some of her spirit there. She'd kept a journal and did so much for her community; I'd find her there and give her stone what life words could conceive on a cold stone in a field of cold stones. Sure, no one would understand but those who knew her, knew her really, but that was all right; in fact, perhaps that would be what is right.

I told my mother about Aster and that I was wanted by the law and the break with Verity and all I hoped to do to beat Verity and to come out clean and it helped so much to say it all like that, to her. I knew what she'd say back, felt her encouragement. She was alive in me and through me. I could almost hear her voice on the autumn wind through the leafless spider leg tree branches and over the gray stones whispering support.

With the sun up and the light turning from auburn to yellow I said goodbye to my mother and the tangible life and walked toward the Manhattan skyline on the western horizon and to the unknown battle to begin in the cyberworld.

Aster flitted about my consciousness bringing mixed amounts of dismay and strength. Scrapes, bruises, and weariness could wait. I had something real to fight for. I came over a rise, the land flattened before falling again to muddled streets and brick buildings and finally to the Brooklyn Bridge.

18

COUNTERATTACK

I MARCHED ACROSS the Brooklyn Bridge like a soldier returning to the front. The bridge's pedestrian walkway is raised above the roadway and goes right down the middle between the traffic coming and going from Manhattan. The morning was bright. I was sticky with cold sweat. My legs were stiff as fence posts. I'd lost the youthful optimism of the young soldier; I'd gained the salty cynicism of the veteran who knew what had to be done and knew his spine was stiff enough to handle incoming artillery while fighting for a chance to bust the enemy lines to fragments, if not for some greater cause, then for his squad.

As I walked I found the desperate struggle heightening my senses. My mental acuity seemed more alive, more aware than ever before. Like a deer tiptoeing in a forest, my senses were tuned to avoid the predators that were somewhere, anywhere. I smelled the salty air wafting from the nearby Atlantic Ocean and the brackish East River and felt the hum of people meandering through this business district just north of Wall Street.

A newspaper box caught my eye. The *New York Post* printed my picture on its front page, while under my photo was the silly caricature of me, the one Verity's system drew with its so-called truth. The headline read: "Online Profiler Strikes Again—Con artist wanted for treason."

So Verity isn't pulling any punches. He has decided to use society, even Big Brother, to hunt me down. What's he so scared of anyway? Me? If that's so, there must be hope.

I looked up at passersby and for a jarring moment felt like a spotlight found me in the crowd, that prison-break alarms were blaring all around. Then I saw the vacant discernment in the eyes of the multitudes along the sidewalks and relaxed. I didn't look like my photo enough for it to matter. I was a tired, weary mess who hadn't shaved in days, and few people look long or hard at someone who is wildly disheveled, someone who'd fallen so far from respectability. Besides, my looks were common. I was still invisible. I had a wallet full of fake IDs. I was nobody in particular.

I bought a newspaper. Shook my head. Choice parts of my profile were listed flatly, like the reporter had no feelings pertaining to the information. They were printed as a computer would, as the reporter only had Verity's profile to work with, not the real me. The sheer coldness of this realization made my hands numb.

As I looked at the article relating my crimes and life, I began to laugh. I didn't expect to; laughing made me feel mad, like a lunatic, until I realized this was a sane response to an insane dilemma. I thought this article proved beyond a doubt I was right. And that was enough, just then.

I tossed the paper and lengthened my stride. I knew what to do.

I found what I needed at New York University's Bobst Library at Washington Square. Getting in was as easy as buying a Friend of the Library membership. I found a private cubbyhole away from curious eyes and eavesdropping ears and plugged in. I disabled the GPS component on my laptop and set up a program to filter my IP address through a proxy server set up by a privacy freak for that purpose in Belgium. I cloaked myself in Triple DES crypto, but took further precautions such as filtering myself through another proxy server in Tokyo.

I looked at Verity's photo again and left the ugly thing open as a window on the screen. This staring, hairless, judgmental countenance was my enemy. How often in life can you look your enemy right in the eyes?

I breathed a deep, long breath before relaxing just a little as I deemed my communications were as safe as I could make them given the time constraints and hardware limitations. I began my assault.

I knew security is only as strong as the weakest link in the chain. This gave me hope. I'd have to find a weak link in Verity's system fast. I had to find something all of the NSA couldn't find in years of trying. But it wasn't as daunting as all that. He had a few tricks. Some advantages. I wouldn't just hunt Verity, but would set baits to attract my deadly prey. During the previous decade I had developed an arsenal of online weaponry.

My face flushed with thoughts of Aster. But no, I thought, no time to think of Aster. Have to begin.

With a deep sigh, I entered the dark side of the Web. The next steps in this desperate battle would carry me over a line, to where the cybercriminals steal, deface, and eavesdrop, to a place I previously only entered with e-tracking software and with the gray areas of the law on my side. But then, I was already a wanted criminal, a cornered animal. I'd been driven to this desperation. Now they could deal with me in this arena.

My first stops were hacker chats where I picked up some Trojan horses. Black Orifice and its cousins—programs I could modify. I downloaded other e-tracking software, cross-site scripting programs, rootkit programs, and more to help create a back door into a system. It's a sticky black market, but I know the players, the deceivers; I know how to prevent someone from sending me an e-bomb or spyware slipped in.

Next, I began digging into my hard drive. The worm, or whatever Verity planted in the NSA via my laptop, was there somewhere. When something is deleted, it isn't necessarily gone. It just becomes less accessible. A search may not turn it up, but it's fairly clean until it is overwritten a time or two. I kept searching for code I didn't recognize. Hours passed before I found something. I blinked. It was gone. I kept digging and swore I saw the code alter before my eyes.

Must be too tired, I thought, but then there it was again.

Could it be? Is this possible?

Then I saw the code change again and knew it was a living worm programmed to evade. There were bits of the worm, the virus, whatever the thing was, all over. Once I knew what to look for I began to see the virus. I started to write it down on a legal pad. Ingenious. It needed a key to be activated, then it combined and sent the requested information along as bits piggybacking on normal packets of info—emails and all the chatter computers do to connect and to log on to the net. When I checked to see the code, it slipped away like an earthworm down a hole. This was it. This was how Verity knew so much. He didn't know everything all at once, but had to search and wait as his virus combined and sent bits of information and then split up again.

The information would go where ordered. Verity didn't need a bank of servers or even any particular computer. He just needed to send out the commands and these sort of modified, insidious shopbots, this malware that had likely infected everything, found the intel and sent it to him where he could then use it to assemble a profile on anyone. It used an invisible style of high-speed word search for anything associated with say, a name, a Social Security number, or another means of identification. It might take minutes or it might take months for the intel to ride out on regular communications through ports, past filters looking for whole viruses, not tiny broken bits of genetic code. This worm could quietly steal from the IRS, from Microsoft, from a DMV. It could get private emails, videos, and phone conversations from cell phones.

Verity, or his Truth Seekers, had developed a new way of synthesizing data. It was so basic, yet so perfect, so invisible. No wonder the NSA was stumped. Without the original code hiding in a deleted section of my hard drive, I wouldn't have seen it either, and even then it was only luck and a trained eye honed from a decade of coding and hunting hackers within all sorts of computer languages and networks that helped me see down the wormhole. The damn thing looked like static, like tiny coding mistakes, but there was a pattern. It was definitely designed.

All I needed was the key to its encryption. If I got it I could use the worm that was everywhere by then to begin sending me data. If I managed that I'd have Verity's system at my bidding. Then I knew how dangerous this was. If public, everyone could use this basic protein virus to see anything they wanted, at least until security measures could be altered to recognize and block it . . . if they could? It would become a war of antidote versus virus, as each was genetically altered to stay ahead of the other.

This told me the other part of his plan was critical. I needed to bait in Verity or one of the Truth Seekers—someone with the key. I decided the only one who was certain to have it was Verity, so I'd have to go straight for the cult leader. Then I'd have to quietly invade Verity's system, to pick his pocket.

I had to try to speak to Verity.

I drew a deep breath and decided not to think, just to jump.

I switched the camera on the computer back on. I tilted the screen on my laptop back far enough so that the camera couldn't see my hands on the keyboard.

I turned on Aster's laptop and set it on my lap. I placed an old piece of gum I found stuck to the bottom of one of the library's desks on the camera atop the screen on Aster's computer. I opened multiple windows on her laptop to watch the proxy servers stripping out my IP address. I knew the attack would begin there, that the NSA could and would overcome those measures. But it would take the NSA time. I knew Verity wouldn't have to overcome this security, as his virus was in my laptop's code. Also, I was sure a data-file sharing program was hidden somewhere on my laptop. There had to be, as this was the only way Verity could put his eyes on the screen so fast, could instantly begin watching me. This laptop had been given to me after all. Someone must have hidden the program where my virus scanner wouldn't see it; the program was likely somewhere in the proprietary code.

It should take some time for Verity's virus to give away my location. I just didn't know how fast the virus could reveal my location. But there wasn't time for caution. It was time to go all in.

I sent emails to Aster's accounts saying I was online and looking for her. I saw the emails pop into the accounts on her laptop. I checked my email accounts and emailed myself meaningless messages. I was trying to get the Truth Seekers' attention. Certainly they'd still be using their system, their virus, to see if I popped up again, to see if they could get me picked up or worse.

I emailed Rooney: "Rooney: I'm ready to turn myself in, if you're willing to work with me. There is a lot I can tell you about Verity. –Sidney"

Rooney's reply was almost instantaneous: "Sidney: You can't escape us. Call me NOW. We'll come and get you. We have Aster. She's talking. We know about the treason. I can't make you promises. But I'll see what I can do if you turn yourself in now. –Rooney"

I watched for the invasion. The NSA's attack came first. It was predictable and obvious. Hundreds of their cyberwarriors were doing all the textbook stuff. They were trying to track my location and invade my system. They first began attacking the remailer I'd used to filter out my email's IP address. Didn't they know who I am?

Some other NSA geek tried to walk right through my email's cryptography but found the "secret" trapdoor closed. They couldn't get through my network security because I was using an algorithm without a trapdoor designed for the NSA. They had no imagination. But I knew in the end they would get through the proxies and cloaking software and find me. They had the talent and the tools. They just had so much bureaucracy to navigate. They were following the codebook when this called for creative hacking.

Verity's attack, however, was almost invisible. Invasion detection software, now programmed to see Verity's virus, soon began giving warnings. Normal pings from programs active and talking to the network were sending out bits of my info. It was like being eaten by ants. They wouldn't get to my heart for a while, but they'd rip off a small piece at a bloody time.

I hoped this meant Verity was online and watching and not just that his virus was alive, always alive.

I was betting Verity wouldn't be capable of resisting talking to me. Verity's ego, after all, was Napoleonic. Anyone who taunted the NSA before profiling politicians, before attacking Big Brother, had hubris. That was a weakness. And because he was an ideologue, Verity would want to twist the knife, to be right. He would have to tell me he was the better man. Verity didn't like that he'd been seen, that I had room to be self-righteous. Verity liked being a teacher. Indeed, this laptop was loaded with spyware from the Truth Seekers. Verity shouldn't have a problem talking to me, as he'd done at the Truth Seekers' "gatherings."

I prepared to record any conversation that might transpire. I needed intelligence. The more info I could gather the better the chance I had of finding a clue that could lead me to Verity. But as I got ready, Verity's eyes flashed on my screen.

I was shell-shocked. I'd hoped for this, but couldn't prepare mentally for it. The glare was reptilian—piercing, emotionless, unblinking cold-blooded eyes cut through me.

I almost fell into a trance, a veritable deer in the headlights of an eighteen-wheeler coming for me, coming to reduce me to nothing. Then Verity's voice rumbled from the laptop's speakers, a deep monotone dripping with suppressed anger. "Did you see enough? Do you know me now? Have you taken enough of me?"

Verity paused and began again with more control: "So you've seen my face. People love mystery, but they always try to define it away, to see enough so they can fit someone into a stereotype. Once they do this they feel safe again. Because once someone is categorized they become see-through; that person falls into a certain clique and takes on the rest of that subset's characterizations as far as they're concerned. I'm sorry that you're just one of the contemptuous, scared little people who have to use stereotypes to fill in the gaps where your mind can't see."

I glared back into those blinking eyes floating on the screen.

Seeing quiet contempt rebounding in my glare, Verity turned venomous: "You're a fool. They're hunting you, yet you think they're right. They don't care about you. They only want to control the populace; they only want power. Are politicians not weighed and rewarded for their deceit and backroom maneuvers, which are only loosely connected to their intellect and ideas? We are in a democracy that reacts to information that is never truly accurate. The press is used and fed and fattened with skill, manipulation, and favors. And journalists spin the news to their own agendas and politics. Percentages and polls can be computed in any direction to prove any point. Meanwhile, Big Brother grows stronger."

As Verity attacked, I regained my bearings.

"Imagine a system that knows not of politics and prejudice, but only facts—facts that you can judge for yourself. A system that knows so well, that people fear to do ill, because there is no escaping their actions. Live boldly. Enjoy your roles. Live them fully and truthfully. Those are the rules of life."

As Verity spoke with the passion of a televangelist, I opened another window on my laptop. I kept my eyes up and worked out of view of Verity's reptilian glare.

When Verity paused, I knew I had to keep him talking, so I said, "Do you mean you don't just want to categorize, but also to control, judge, and shape?"

Verity took the bait. "You want the perfect person. I'll show him to you. He's not so rare, you know. The problem is he or she is so hard to see, to catch. Perfection is invisibility. When a person perfectly fits his or her role, they are married to their background, intertwined with it, part of it. They're not a man or woman at their crowning moment, but a person in their crowning moment. They're in the colors and the background, the sound and the action. They're the conductor and the orchestra. And they know it. They don't use it to shove their worth down the throats of others. They don't hold perfection up and say 'look at what I've done.' They're perfection. And they move with the scene. Yes, their scene. And it's all they have ever wanted. Perhaps you've felt that way for a fleeting moment when playing sports, or video games, or programming. Such moments come when we completely lose touch with the physical and therefore control the physical; it's a Zen master's dream. And it happens. It's the farmer plowing perfect rows. The teacher so in tune with his pupils he can feel their pulses beating along together. The lawyer who doesn't hear herself speaking but sees the jurors swaying.

The officer who feels the street scene around him as with his fingertips, sensing all of the relationships and interactions. And, above all, the perfect person knows that this is the perfection of his or her role; the role they've longed to perfect. This is how the system will put people in their proper place."

Jabbing, looking to keep Verity talking as I hacked his system, I said, "You'd categorize everyone. What about the pegs that don't fit?"

Verity bobbed out of the question's way: "No, now is the time for the system. It's being created all around us already. Technology has outpaced privacy, and now it is the individuals who suffer. Landlords can see detailed accounts of your renting and financial history. Credit unions have files on everyone. Medical records are going digital. Criminal records, stock trading, buying tendencies . . . if you do something the information can, and likely is, being categorized and sold. Big Brother is not just government any longer, but industry as well; the line is being blurred between the two. This is why it's time for Big Brother to be de-robed, run out of town. It's time for people to use truth to level the playing field, to make a world where everyone is accountable to their actions—government and industry included. Unless the public gains access to the truth by fully releasing it, they will be controlled and manipulated like no other time in history . . ."

"Preaching truth, so-called facts spun out of context!"

Verity said, "I'm sorry I wasted my time teaching you . . . maybe if I had gotten to you younger." For a moment Verity sounded sad. The teacher in Verity was still strong; however, the shift in tone made me realize Verity had said what he wanted to say and so was about to sign off.

I jabbed, "I've seen your truth. I read my profile. It's not me. You don't have my soul. You really think you're creating the Garden of Eden?"

Verity's eyes tightened as I hacked. Hacking is not a method; it's a creative process. You try an idea, fail, but learn. Then you try again. The trick is to gather intelligence without letting them know what's going on, and to avoid being followed home. I hoped to do this by modifying Verity's worm so it would allow pieces of software to piggyback into Verity's system. It would then carry and reassemble a keylogger program, software that would read and report Verity's keystrokes to me. I was laying the groundwork to steal Verity's encryption key to control the virus. This would take time. I didn't know if I could keep Verity talking long enough, or if Verity would get me first.

Verity's eyes flitted down then up again and he said, "Foolish boy. No, this open system won't be a biblical Eden. Eden is denial. Eden is living without knowledge. Eden, the sanctuary before the sin of eating the Fruit of Knowledge, which brought the first guilt—the guilt of nakedness, of the body, shame at our own appearance. Eden uses a recipe of ignorance from appearance. Which is good, the flesh shouldn't shape the mind, but its key ingredient is wrong. Simple ignorance is not utopian—it's death. Becoming a dumb animal unaware of ourselves is not our key to Eden. A dog trusting in a provider, begging for every bone, is not enlightenment. Eden, the true Eden, is quite the opposite."

I repressed a smile as I had a connection to Verity's computer. In moments I used the modified worm to slip a keystroke program into Verity's hard drive.

When the malware was all in, I uploaded Black Orifice, a program that would give me the key to a back door into Verity's PC.

"The only way to find penance from our 'Original Sin' is through absolute knowledge. A total abhorrence of appearance can be had only with the absolute knowledge of what's inside . . ."

When Black Orifice was in and running I walked into Verity's hard drive. I recognized the computer languages and the software used. My face flushed slightly as a deeper vulnerability occurred to me.

Verity paused and really looked at me a moment. His eyes went down, then back to mine. He was watching a data-analysis program that was reading my emotions from my eye dilation, skin temperature, nostril flare, and the expressions on my face. Verity knew I was hacking him.

I did my best to deaden my expression. I'd seen that my best attack on this system was to use a cross-site scripting program. But I had to keep this off my face.

Verity's eyes widened a moment, then went back to normal as he said, "You're still my pawn, Sidney. I have you profiled. I know all . . ."

Yes, stay arrogant you scum, I thought. I knew a good security patch hadn't yet been written for this weakness. I'd busted a hacker the month before who'd cross-site scripted her way into a subsidiary company's billing department. Her Manhattan-based headquarters audited its subsidiaries on a partially shared network. She'd used this oversight access to transfer funds to a fictitious contractor she'd created by changing the operating system's passwords and then wiring the funds bundled with a thousand others. The weakness she'd exploited hadn't yet been widely reported, as the company was still fixing its software glitches. Verity's Truth Seekers were cutting-edge worm writers sure enough, but they weren't in my league when it came to security measures. I initiated the cross-site scripting attack by launching the software from my waiting arsenal through the open port.

"So you think you're God?"

If eyes could scowl, Verity's did. "No, not me. The system, however, will come as close to God as we've ever come."

I still didn't know Verity's original IP address. Verity was talking through proxies. No matter. I'd have everything soon. I next uploaded a rootkit program into Verity's system. I embedded this program in the computer's operating system, a place I knew Verity's security software wasn't programmed to look. My fingers then danced over the keyboard as I used the rootkit to make myself the system's administrator. I changed the passwords from within the operating system and required the operating system's kernel, the central component of the system, to interface with a shell program I installed via the rootkit. This gave me complete access and control of Verity's computer, if I chose to use this access. The catch was that Verity's computer would have to be turned on and logged on to the net before I could log in to search the hard drive or to change settings.

Verity stopped preaching as his glare shifted.

Has he found my location?

Regardless, I needed more time.

"God, absolute knowledge, a world without privacy? The people in your Eden would be afraid to be people. Everything they'd do and say would first be weighed by how others might perceive the action. You wouldn't save the individual; you'd condemn her. From birth people would be more worried about shaping their profiles than becoming who they should be. You'd have a million drones and a few outcasts."

Verity eyes seemed disappointed. "You're still very young, aren't you? You understand so little . . ."

The back door into Verity's system only gave me a way into the computer Verity was then using. I still had to find and get into his profiling database, the server or cloud account he was using to build and house the profiles he'd use during the debate. I assumed Verity must be logging into this server remotely. The other Truth Seekers helping to build the database must be doing the same thing. For security reasons, Verity wouldn't house that database on his own system. Only an amateur would make that error. It was just as easy to log on to a server remotely, whether a zombie computer or a paid-for portion of a host's server. To get this, I'd have to wait for Verity to log on to the remote server. The keylogger program would then record Verity's passwords. With the back door installed, I would then get access to his system. But I'd have to hope Verity logged on.

I said, "You'll destroy individual expression."

Verity's voice rattled from the bottom of his cynical chest: "I'll pluck you from the true path like a weed. In Eden, the true Eden, people will finally be whoever they want to be, without interference from others who are jealous of their ability. Talent is self-evident. Appearance is irrelevant. People won't say that she's pretty, but that she is a great chemical engineer."

"'Great' sounds like a perception to me. But do you really think a man will ignore a pair of well-shaped legs to wonder what she's really like underneath?"

"Not on the street, where everyone is a stranger, but in the workplace where they'd admire something else."

I smiled haughtily and said, "Have you ever worked in an office? Have you any idea the amount of backstabbing and gossip you'd be feeding? Only a saint would be free of persecution. And a saint might be mocked for being a prude. Do you really think a random list of facts can explain flesh, reasoning, angst?"

Verity's anger deepened. "Blasphemy! Nothing is perfect in this disorderly world, but it can be so much better. There is so much bias and racism that we can erase if we look deeper. If we know everything, if we can decipher each person, then I can tell what they want, think, and will do. I can put each person in their proper place."

I lashed back as I completed the hack: "Sounds to me like you're perfecting racism. Instead of skin tone and religious affiliation you'll be stereotyping according to hobbies, test scores, internet buying tendencies, Google searches."

Verity said, "People don't change. They learn. And though there will be exceptions, the law of averages—"

"I thought this was perfect for each individual?"

"You fool, humility will restrain the populace. People will be afraid to do ill. Each individual can be helped, herded, educated according to the means of their talents."

"Late bloomers be damned."

Verity's system was compromised.

Verity said, "The system will take them into account. Nothing is absolute. But they will have to live with themselves. In the future they will learn and will be afraid to be—".

"Individuals!".

"Damn you," said Verity. "You want to see what Big Brother can do, watch this?"

Verity's eyes disappeared and Aster's face appeared all washed out from tears.

19

BIG BROTHER'S REVENGE

I GRABBED MY laptop's screen and squeezed it in the quiet cubbyhole of the Manhattan library. I wanted to reach right through the screen and to pull Aster away from them.

A close-up of Aster's darling face filled the laptop's screen, only she was anything but darling then. Her hair was tied back and greased. Electronic probes stuck to her scalp and read the beats of her troubled heart. A head and neck brace held her still. White light overexposed her skin. She stared straight out the monitor at whomever was questioning her with their cameras and computer programs reading her, raping her of her thoughts, desires, and deceits, of herself.

Then, somewhere in front of Aster, Special Agent Rooney demanded, "Now Nancy, tell me, where is Sidney?"

"I told you a thousand times, I don't know," she said as her voice trailed off into her lost heart.

"What was his plan, his intentions?"

"To fuck you!"

Rooney said, "Ah, now Nancy, you're gonna have to talk to us. We're here to help you. We are your government. We're duly elected to protect you. Don't you understand that? This Verity is a criminal. He emailed us your profile. We know everything about you. He sold you out. He's not your friend. There's no reason to protect him. Help us. We'd hate to have to make all this information on you public."

Aster managed to say as weariness made her nose shiver, her lips quiver, "How? I don't know. I've never met Verity. I don't know who he is. I don't know where Sidney is. I don't know anything."

"We'll be the judge of that."

Just as I again tried to murder my computer, I was yanked back into the living scene by laughter.

I jolted up from my horror and saw some students passing nearby. They were joshing one another about something. But they'd slapped me awake. I wiped my eyes, and knew, suddenly was sure, Verity was trying to stall me. By now Verity's slow-but-sure virus would have gathered enough to determine my location.

Nausea flooded me as I shut down the laptops, killing the connection to Aster, who was somewhere, being raped of everything that was her.

I stuffed the laptops into my computer bag and slung the bag over my head and left shoulder. I marched through the library on the balls of my feet. I didn't know what to do next. I only knew I'd better get out and fast. The last layer of my connection was a wireless service in the library. As I lengthened my stride I thought maybe I should just wait for them. Maybe I'd be better off in their hands while I still had something to bargain with, that I couldn't possibly win this battle anyway. Who was I but a nonperson, a homeless fool, a criminal?

I thought, *Maybe if they had me they'd be easier on Aster*. But I knew that wasn't true and conceded, no, they'd be worse; they'd have nothing to lose and everything to gain.

This library was a convenient place to work, but was also a trap. There was only one exit. I lowered my head as I neared a camera at the door. I began to walk through sensors designed to detect metallic strips in library books, a system so stupid you could beat it with a magnet, when I saw wingtips stop. A suit was in my way. I started to sidestep when a steel grip seized my arm.

"Hello, Sidney," said Special Agent Bent. "Rooney, would like to see you, you fucking little traitor."

I didn't resist. Bent outweighed me by fifty pounds of muscle.

Instead I simply said, "Hello, Bent. You're sweating. You didn't run all the way here on my account?"

Bent's grip tightened more than I thought possible as he towed me like a dog on a leash.

Bent led me outside and down a sidewalk toward a waiting car at the end of the block. Car doors were opening.

"I'm not a traitor."

"Save it."

"Oh, you don't think, you just follow orders, huh?"

"That's right."

"At least I'm on the right side."

Bent stopped, looked at me as if I were a bug. "Right side."

"Freedom's."

"Bullshit," said Bent as his grip loosened, just a little.

I suddenly twisted my arm toward Bent's thumb and pivoted my hips as I kicked him in the balls.

I came loose as Bent fell to his knees. But just for a moment. Then his arms were wrapped around my chest.

Other agents were out of the car, coming.

I pulled down as Bent violently pulled up to control me. Then I bounded up by kicking my knees up into my chest and our momentum worked together.

We toppled.

Bent landed on his back with me on top. The fall broke us apart.

I was up and running.

Footsteps stomped chaotically behind. Cries and blasts of air in to and out of lungs ricocheted off glass buildings. Hands reached into jackets and pulled out semiautomatic handguns. I dug my toes into the sidewalk and ran as if a lion were after me. There was no trickery, no dodging in and out of buildings, just an endurance match. I wasn't a fighter. I'd only learned a little judo from a friend. But I am a fine middle-distance runner. I'd run the eight-hundred meter in 1:52 in high school. I still ran. I found it burned off angst, conquered myself, gave me peace. The men chasing me lifted weights instead. They could crush my bones with their arms. They could sprint. But they couldn't outpace me in a distance run.

Blocks blurred by. Soon I was too far ahead for them to see. I melted into the crowd. Took side streets. And was gone.

As I cradled the laptop bag in my left arm like a football and swung my right arm as I ran, an idea shook loose.

20

THE HAIL MARY SHOT

I WENT INTO a subway station at Canal Street and West Broadway and took a number 2 train north to 72nd Street and Broadway. I climbed up out of the subway station under a blue sky and walked east two blocks to Central Park. I slowed a little after I crossed Central Park West's traffic. I slumped down in a tree's shadow with my back against a maple and my butt on damp fallen leaves and watched traffic honking past on the busy street.

My mind settled as sweat turned cold on my skin. I recalled I'd once heard someone speak with the same cadence, with the same word choices Verity used. The cult leader's style and thought pattern were familiar, somehow. Or did it just seem so because he was so accent-free, so generic? I wasn't sure as I looked up into falling yellow maple leaves. But I knew there had to be a way to find out.

I recalled a study done by an Oxford professor who proved Shakespeare had written all the plays attributed to him. Whether one man could have written all the plays said to be authored by Shakespeare was then being debated by a few respected academics. Their contention was that one man would not have had the time to write all those plays in the span of years they were known to have been written. But then a professor's program proved, based on word usage and voice, that they had to have been penned by the same mind—Shakespeare wasn't just a genius, he was a hardworking genius.

I picked up a twig and snapped it in two. I knew evaluating word choices is a complex process only made possible by sophisticated software. It was more of an art than a science; still, such a hunt is especially possible in English. Because English is the largest and most diverse language, people can be more eclectic with their word choices. According to the *Oxford English Dictionary* there are at least 600,000 words in the English language. Now most people only use about 30,000 of them, but some minds may use a quarter of the language. Indeed, constructing sentences for a writer is an art form, an expression of their voice. It is especially possible to see and hear a stylistic writer's voice, but everyone has variations. These variations can act as fingerprints, indicated the study.

Some MIT students had turned that professor's program into a tool for rooting out plagiarists a dozen years before. One of my professors explained the mathematical method that made it possible. I knew the program was out there somewhere on the Web. The NSA shut the tool down by classifying it; however, some students kept the software online and sent it to different sites with various names.

I'd seen the program online. I'd even taken precautions not to let a program like it find me on the net, as it occurred to me that a program that searched emails for particular thought patterns could conceivably find a person, even a person deep undercover, by reading emails and comparing them to known written records. It would just take the right math; like matching a fingerprint, it would need enough consistency to find likely matches.

The program was listed on some hacker sites. It had been called various appellations to keep NSA cyberwarriors from finding it with basic keyword searches. I didn't have time, access, or the hardware to do an Echelon-style search of all communications for emails to see who might be a likely match for Verity. I supposed the NSA had tried that big dragnet with their Total Information Awareness Program fruitlessly by then anyway; however, I knew it wasn't really necessary for me to go through all that hassle; instead, I'd follow my online nose; I'd do what a good cop would do: I'd sift through people who had the right profiles.

So then, what kind of person is Verity likely to be?

I left the park and walked west to a Starbucks on Columbus Avenue and stood right next to a newspaper rack loaded with papers showcasing a photo snapped of me the day the FBI picked me up. I ignored what amounted to wanted posters and ordered a large coffee. I liked calling it "large," not the pretentious "Venti." I thought myself anti-establishment enough to disdain false refinement. And so I simply smiled when the person in the green smock scoffed, "Oh, you mean *Venti*?"

I found a seat in a corner lounge chair where I could watch the store's patrons. I popped open my laptop and set it on a small, round table. I turned off my computer's camera and turned on my cryptography. I made sure my security software was completely updated and therefore able to prevent Verity's virus from sneaking out my whereabouts. I knew I couldn't completely beat Verity's virus, as it was in the basic code where it would take more time to eradicate. But as long as I slowed it down, I'd be relatively safe for a while. I just didn't know for how long.

I logged on through the café's wireless network. I checked to see what keystrokes Verity had been typing.

Nothing yet.

I did a keyword search for the MIT students who'd written the program. A copy of the author-identity program showed up on a German porn site. I almost laughed. It seemed some of the students were privacy activists. They were fighting Big Brother by continuously posting this and many other programs on unlikely websites around the globe.

I downloaded the program. As I viewed its formula and code I remembered it like a book I'd read long ago and forgotten. It came back from my deep memory and I altered the program slightly by updating its dictionary with the Urban Dictionary, so that it knew street speak such as circle jerk, chavs, and camel toe, and a Netlingo.com's dictionary so it knew that 143 was "I love you" and ADIH was "another day in hell."

Once the program was up to date, I loaded in Verity's conversations and wondered who he could be. Who could I compare Verity's word choices and sentence structure to? I started with politicians, by finding their speeches online, and then I found online speeches and blogs from Silicon Valley gurus. Soon it was late afternoon and I was getting nowhere.

I went for another coffee. I glanced at the news rack and my photo as I waited. I thought my photo wasn't me at all. The thing looked too weak for a man taking on the government and a super villain all in one day. Then my eyes fell to another headline: "Last Presidential Debate Tonight."

That's right, the last presidential debate was scheduled for 8:00 p.m. tonight at Madison Square Garden.

I'd forgotten about the debate. I'd even forgotten about the presidential election. I sat back down in a comforter at Starbucks and felt caffeine giving my exhausted body light tremors. I closed my eyes. Dizziness spun me around. I felt as if I were drunk on a merry-go-round. I opened my eyes. Shook my head. No time for rest. I had to clear my head. There was no time for mistakes. I could be wrong, but this was my best shot. I had to get into the presidential debate.

I more felt than knew the debate was where Verity planned to go public, to kill Big Brother. And I was sure Verity would be there. It was his pattern. He had even been in Grand Central Station when he spoke to me. Verity liked to personally taunt the NSA, the FBI. He liked to be at the center of things. He was like a serial killer who shows up at victims' funerals.

The idea occurred to me that, like some serial killers, maybe he even wanted to be caught, but this train of thought derailed when an alert flashing on my laptop's screen told me Verity was logging on. This was my chance. I opened a window on my laptop and watched keystrokes coming in through the keylogger program I'd hidden in Verity's hard drive.

"*Bam!*" I said, causing some Manhattanite in a too-tight Gap shirt to stare at me.

The password is "AllTheMenMerePlayers2/7." Verity's a Shakespeare fan, I half thought and half whispered.

I followed Verity into his system by using the password. As I slipped in I reminded myself that I needed to keep a low profile. I needed my intrusion not to be detected. Ideally, I'd wait until the wee hours to sneak in when no one was logged on, but there wasn't time for such practical thievery. I had to be bold.

I checked the surroundings. I saw that whoever set this up did a sloppy job. All of the DSL internet connections were cloaked with something that resembled BlackICE Defender, but they were using a rudimentary password system. And so many ports. So many. No doubt they needed them so the packets of info from Verity's virus could seep in like water through a sieve.

I noticed that stuff was coming from everywhere. My vulnerability scanning software was showing all sorts of open ports. This isn't a system at all. Just like I guessed, it's a new way of synthesizing data. Unreadable bits are coming from everywhere and connecting here. But they could just as well connect elsewhere, if a person had the right codes, the right algorithm to reassemble them. The whole internet is his system. I'm not sure how to kill this thing. It's a virus. But so basic. It's like a common protein.

My mind raced along as I explored Verity's system. There were so many different caricatures of politicians. All drawn in cartoon fashion—like a political cartoonist's fantasyland. Striped three-piece suits have greedy looks; politicians with toothy grins and pay slots by their ears; doctors happily, furiously signing prescriptions, so many, all with the same name . . . but each was different, somehow tailored to each individual's photo and changed to include their character traits. Like the ones I saw in Grand Central.

Yes, yes, look at the formula. Information comes in, is keyed to a certain profile, and then fed into a mathematical formula—here let me copy it, okay—the program does all the work. I was right, that's how one man, or a small group of people, can do so much. They just apply a formula to every person and let the computer do the work. Using shopbots and scanners, small parcels that go out and feed unseen, it even gathers its own intelligence and changes the profile as info is added. So simple.

I kept plowing through the network, exploring, hoping curiosity wouldn't be the death of me. I looked at file dates and saw that journalists and politicians were then being actively profiled. Both presidential candidates were there as well as all of Congress and so many more.

Then a revelation, of course, the Truth Seekers are the hackers I was after. That was why there was no mole to be found on the inside of that company. They'd found a way to take what they wanted. That's how they paid for all those laptops and software and for who knows what else. They found a way to make all the money they need online by using insider-trading info to buy and sell the right stocks. Verity was self-righteous, but he was really just a very successful super villain, a sophisticated thief.

All that better-than-thou stuff was from a hypocrite. How disappointingly typical.

I finally leaned back and sucked a breath that ballooned my chest, then exhaled as I realized this was obviously a database being built for a purpose, for the presidential debate. I reasoned my intrusion hadn't yet been detected because there were ten other active users in this intranet database. I saw them by their online names—Jungle Jim, Land Shark, Net Guru, Tron . . . Some were popping in and out as they poured in more intel. Their IP addresses were all stripped via proxy servers. They were getting ready for something.

I didn't dare move large bits of info out of this network. If I had their packet sniffers and intrusion-detection software would alert them they were being hacked. Instead, I loaded in Trojan horses with cross-site scripting software, which I hoped would allow me to inject script. Then I entered the security portion of their network and smiled. I'd written a good portion of the code for this system for IBM. I'd even given security recommendations to their code writers. I knew this system and its vulnerabilities. I put in new passwords and turned off some of the intrusion-detection capabilities. I then designed a security protocol that would later allow me to shut out the other users by simply logging in remotely on my laptop and altering the firewalls.

After an hour of setting up this system, I decided there was a way to really hedge my bets, but first I'd need a throwaway cell phone. I shut my laptop and hurried to a corner store.

The phone rang six times before an angry man's voice demanded, "Who the hell is this and how the fuck did you get this private number?"

"Do you want revenge on Verity, Senator?"

His voice exploded, "How can you give me revenge?"

"I'm Sidney McDaniel."

Senator Harris said, "What is it you have?"

"I know how to take down Verity. All I need is a little help from you."

Senator Harris growled, decided not to lose his temper, and said, "Me? Why haven't you called the FBI?"

"I'm wanted by the FBI."

"I know."

"I want my freedom back. At the same time I can get you yours. Or I can call someone else."

"And if I call the FBI?"

"They won't catch me. And regardless, if they do, none of this will come out. They'll use Verity's system for their own ends, as will presidents. Your name will never be completely cleared if that happens."

"I don't follow. What is it that you can do?"

"I've seen Verity's face. I've been in his system. I need more information for his profile. You're speaking at the debate tonight. With your help, I can reveal him to the public. I can destroy him."

Senator Harris's voice quaked, "I'll need proof."

I was prepared for that. "Turn on your computer, Senator. Log on to your congressional email account."

A minute of fumbling passed before Harris said, "Now what?"

"Whose soul do you want to see?"

Senator Harris didn't hesitate: "The president of the United States."

Two minutes later Harris worried aloud, "If that thing gets out it'll overshadow all of us. He did skip military service, huh. The man who went in his place was killed in action . . ."

"Now my part of the bargain, Senator. I need you to email me everything you have on Verity. Everything Agent Rooney gave you. Everything you have access to. All the background. All the conversations. Everything. Then I need you to meet me . . ."

21

PREPARING FOR THE LAST BATTLE

A METICULOUSLY DRESSED salesman at Brooks Brothers on Madison Avenue and 44th ran his eyes up and down my gritty figure as he nasally exhaled, "Oh Lord, no." Then the salesman's chin fell to his palm and his manicured fingers tapped his powdered cheek. He said, "Another off-the-rack waste wondering where he can find the closest Sears."

The salesman strutted between racks of suits with his nose elevated above a salmon tie. He stopped in front of me and said, "Can I help you, you poor-looking little thing? You look like you've been living on the streets in that polyester parody, you know."

I said, "Yeah, you'll do. I need to look great tonight."

"Do we now?"

The salesman put his hands on his hips.

"Spare no expense."

The salesman blushed from joy, then probed along my waist and arms with a cloth tape measure. "Oh, goodie, a solid build with sexy lines. You're going to be a fun project."

As I walked into a fitting room I corrected him: "No, not a clean canvas, but an assignment. I'm going to the presidential debate tonight and I need to look dignified."

"Oh, a conservative look then," said the salesman as his nose crinkled and fingers that had never formed a proper fist tapped his clean chin.

"Yes, a starchy part to play."

The salesman who preferred the title "stylist" used only his thumb and pointer finger to pull garments as he talked to himself as much as he did to me. "I must admit, I judged you harshly. You dress like an off-the-rack nobody, you know. And clothes do more than make the man, they define the man."

"Yes," I said, "I've heard the old Mark Twain line: 'Clothes make the man. Naked people have little or no influence on society.'"

"Joke if you like," said the salesman, "but clothes shield us in foppery or finery for the scenes of our lives. So few understand the importance of image. We can't just be who we want to be, we have to portray who we want to be; if we don't others will just discount and define us before we're able to show them our true colors underneath."

I smiled more broadly than I had in days and said as the salesman handed me a suit to try, "If you only knew."

After an hour of sizing, tailoring I walked out in a Madison Saxxon pinstripe with silver cuff links, a red-blue striped silk tie, cordovan loafers, and an assertive stride. I was ready to take on the world, or be buried in style.

Next stop, a pharmacy. I bought Ciba Vision's FreshLook colored contacts. I chose a hazel blend, as they matched Aster's. I also purchased Pearl Vision's Converse Energy frames, as they were heavy enough to fool the facial-recognition software that would certainly be guarding the entrance. I knew facial-recognition software relies on a very basic mathematical formula that measures the distance between the eyes and adds it to 128 other facial proportions. It then statistically looks for close matches. Putting on glasses can fool the math. Wearing colored contacts with pupils sized a little larger or smaller can, too. I hedged my bets and did both. If I'd had more time, I would have added larger cheekbones, maybe a more pronounced nose. But that kind of makeup would take hours.

I didn't think they'd have biometric scanners, such as Indentix programs. And if they did, I didn't think it would matter. Not even the government had everyone's retinal scan and fingerprints on file, at least not yet. And this was a large, public event. But then, I presumed they had my biometrics. I figured this was one of the things they took when Special Agent Rooney first had me picked up and questioned. And if not, they surely got my biometrics when I went to the NSA's headquarters. Doing so isn't difficult. This was a risk I'd have to take. I just hoped the sheer size of the event along with my precautions would allow me to slip through the digital dragnet.

I went to a barbershop. I tipped heavily to get in without an appointment and had my hair buzzed on the sides and back and lopped short enough on top to look like a former serviceman who'd been taught that hair is only a bother. I also had a shave, then saw myself in a mirror and almost didn't recognize the man staring back. I'd always worn my hair long enough to style, as it made playing different parts more possible. But I liked this conservative look. I just hoped it would be enough to fool the FBI agents and anyone who'd seen a newspaper or a news program.

Back in a coffee shop, with two hours to go, my fingers beat a steady rhythm on my laptop's keyboard. I had a lot of programming to do. I wasn't sure if I could pull this off. The emails from Senator Harris were loaded with info, but also a lot of guesswork. I'd leave out the assumptions from the team of FBI profilers. I needed raw info, not generalizations and expert assumptions. Only the truth would bite to the marrow. I used Verity's profiling program to build a profile of him by using everything I could get, including the photo I had of Verity. I added in our last conversation, which caused Verity's caricature to change in an amusing way I hoped he wouldn't find so comical.

To keep my movements from Verity's prying eyes, I used Tor, a router sponsored by the Electronic Frontier Foundation that would help anonymize my Web traffic by bouncing it between volunteer servers. I also downloaded software called the Cloak, a free program that sits like a firewall between a PC and the Web to prevent others from obtaining your IP address. The Cloak also uses the standard SSL protocol to encrypt communications from browsers, so I hoped all that would stall Verity's virus.

I found a schematic of Madison Square Garden on an engineering journal's website. The CAD drawing had been added as a sidebar to an article on the challenges of building a huge multimedia arena, a place that could grow ice overnight for a hockey game, yet somehow could be ready the next day for a rock concert.

The Garden had been renovated over the decades to bring its security and technology up to modern needs. The Garden's multimedia system was just then being upgraded to new HD facilities, including a Sony MVS-8000G HD switcher and a Harris NEXIO server linking multiple Harris Velocity NXes and an Apple Final Cut Studio HD craft edit system. All of this was working on a shared storage network. I was familiar with these systems. And was delighted when I found the primary audio suite featured a new SSL C100 HD digital audio console. They were basing their entire multichannel audio production on the C100 HD (C140/32) console. I saw that the board handled 5.1 surround audio signals that were used to mix full surround sound. The console also handled all of the audio production for the two in-house studios, where the stereo boom mics and wireless lavalier mics were used. I found the system's heart. Now I just had to find a way to get at it.

I was adept at reading engineering schematics, as it was a necessary part of developing a secure intranet system, but I would have liked to have had weeks or even months to prepare for an attack on a closed system as secure as this. But still, their system, though huge, was very basic. I saw several places where I could break into the closed network. That the arena was currently under construction was lucky, as disorder brews possibility.

I took a deep breath, mentally shifted gears. I needed to slip into Verity's system one more time. I hoped I wasn't pushing my luck too far.

I logged back in using the passwords Verity used. I was in easily. I resisted the urge to use the system to see what was happening to Aster, as they'd surely be keeping track of her interrogation. As I thought of her, rage flushed through me and I had to shut my eyes a moment. I ordered myself to follow the plan. I knew there was no time to be distracted by my heart.

A message popped open as a window: "Identify yourself!"

Panic roiled me as I typed, "A Truth Seeker."

"What's your code name?"

I realized I was using Verity's passwords, though Verity likely wasn't logged on just then, so I couldn't hide my movements in Verity's shadow. My mind raced, then took a chance: "Jungle Jim."

"Oh, hi Jim, you must be on a new PC."

"Yes, I'm on the move. Switching according to protocol."

"Yes, yes, of course."

I knew I was lucky they were coming in through proxy servers, as there was no IP address to identify me. I thought the only reason I drew an alert was that I was likely coming through a proxy they weren't then using. I didn't know where their proxies might be.

I thought it likely I'd been saved by their disorganization; their lack of knowledge about even one another.

I uploaded the profile of Verity and replaced other files. The files were in order of topics, as they'd be presented during the debate. I didn't have time to view them; instead I quickly replaced files in the middle of the program . . . fifteen minutes ticked to thirty as files uploaded through my poor connection and proxies and then I was done and wiping my brow, smiling wide.

I then infected the system, wherever it physically was being housed, with a Trojan horse packet filled with viruses. I placed this e-bomb in folders data indicated hadn't been utilized in weeks. It would go off halfway through the debate. It would unleash some of the most sophisticated attacks ever developed by smart, bored, American youth. The system would crash and eat itself, or so I hoped.

I shut down and tried not to think about the impossible mission.

22

BEHIND ENEMY LINES

I LOITERED AT 7th Avenue and 33rd watching every flavor of person passing through the yellow glow of streetlights that cool November evening. People were striding in and out of Penn Station and Madison Square Garden as if the meaning of their lives drew sustenance from that evening's events. This was the pace the city was famous for, its living pulse. I could feel the pressure, smell the testosterone that was so alluring, so addictive it drew people from every part of the globe to this tiny island. I began to wonder whether all this mad activity was just mad, or perhaps if all the miniscule actions in this flurry of beehive activity were all building to some great goal no one bee really understood.

New York's pounding pace made me feel small, inconsequential on this epic night. I no longer felt so arrogantly special in the electrified digital world I was running through, but instead felt as a rat might as it scurried along the tunnels of a scientist's maze. I lingered in relative darkness alongside a building deciding maybe a better metaphor was that I was like one of the nonexistent fleas in a flea circus that supposedly makes merry-go-rounds turn and tiny trapezes swing, miniature rides that actually get all their energy via an electric current from a hidden battery.

I felt the weight of the laptop in my bag and thought of what I'd already planted in the Truth Seekers' system. This made me feel powerful, unique. Yes, I felt bigger than a flea, but I suppressed the feeling of superiority, as it wasn't an honest emotion. It was heady, egotistical; it was blindness and false worth; it was tunnel vision. I must remain humble, human, open-minded. I couldn't let them or my own desires and successes and failures take me from myself. I needed to be myself and nothing more. I needed to go into the battle of my life with a clean mind and open heart. That way I'd come out a winner or a loser but intact regardless.

As I stood still weariness began to pull me down to the cold, gray cement. I'd completed a superhuman amount of work during the past hours and days. I knew my chances of success were still miniscule, even though I'd gotten a series of fortunate breaks. I felt so tired. My burned-out eyes added halos to streetlights. Vertigo shook me.

I looked closer at the people passing to attain purchase as a seasick person does a shoreline. I decided to occupy my mind by attempting to see them as individuals, not as a collective mass. I began to notice them then, to see them truly, to look beyond their costumes, their parts. I saw they all had different expressions, different worries. Few were really alike in dress, walk, and manner. Some, like a blonde knockout in a short black dress and a stiff insecure walk, didn't like themselves. She seemed confused by her looks. They were appealing, which she obviously cherished, but they drew unwanted, not just wanted eyes, which she disdained. She was very confused, a living contradiction. Then a man whose stomach seemed a full stride ahead of his skimpy legs passed. This man let gluttony define him. Then a young woman in a business suit who seemed to know she was wearing a costume to fit into the scene of her choice strode by.

I watched her walk and thought she seemed to understand who she was. I saw that they all were individuals in different chapters of their lives and that their clothes and expressions were shields. It was just that some of them didn't know it. I adored watching them then.

"You having fun, young man?"

The voice was deep and nearby. An image of Special Agent Bent roiled me as I jerked my head right, saw no one, then down. The voice had come from a homeless person, a black man sitting on a crate.

"Yes," I said, relieved I hadn't been caught so stupidly.

The old, homeless man flashed white teeth in the almost darkness near the building as he said, "All these busy drones are fun to watch, all scurrying along while I quietly notice things, important things as the sun rises and falls."

I was surprised and intrigued by the homeless man's educated, reflective choice of thoughts. "You've chosen this part then?"

"Of course. All of us homeless aren't off our rockers, ya know. Some, well, just give up or are beaten down by life, by the system."

"The system?"

"Uh-huh," huffed the homeless man, "I worked thirty years in a mailroom, always running to help some suit get something on time like it really mattered as much as life and death. Then I lost everything one damn day when someone's package went missing. I was accused of stealing. They prosecuted me all right but the bastards couldn't convict me, of course, 'cause I hadn't taken nothin'. But they went and searched my apartment and found a stapler, some pencils, and other trash from the company, so they prosecuted me for stealing that crap and fired me. Now you jus' try an' get a decent job in this city when you're sixty and your back is all busted up and your name is fuckin' thief. Oh sure, I struggled on a long while, welfare, some minimum-wage day jobs, then my wife passed on and I just give up. This society says I'm trash, so I jus' decided to act like the big, black garbage bag they think I am. Now I watch them pass me by and I don't mind, 'cause I finally see what matters. Sounds like shit, but it's the truth; now I jus' regret all those years spent thinkin' gettin' packages on time was my whole reality."

I leaned against the cement building in a shadow of a pillar away from the streetlights and said, "That isn't right."

"You're young ain't you, boy? Hell you'll learn. It ain't about what's right. Everywhere I went they knew who I was. All they had to do was punch it up on a computer. The state done that. No chance. It's all in my record. I'm just another black man with an attitude, a no-good thief. No truth to it, but it doesn't matter, I fit their perception of what I'm supposed to be. No man looked me in the eye and give me a chance. They looked at my state-sanctioned record."

"You've been cast out."

The old man chuckled. "Yeah, that's one way to put it. Now I'm jus' a nonperson. One day I'll be, eh, a John Doe on a slab, yeah that's it, and then burned all up in a state oven and then gone and that's how I want it. They can take your name, you know, and in the end they can take your corpse, but they can't take you unless you hand yourself to them. Sit down, watch, feel, learn, you'll find what's real; I'm not sayin' not to work, to dream, jus' make sure you know what's real, what matters to you. I got more than this street. I got places, not mine, but places to go. But here, hell, I'm me. Try it, jus' stop, watch, after a time you'll see people for who they are, for what they are. You'll find out what you really need ain't much. You'll find out color don't matter, only staying yourself does, only bein' what's right. Maybe I'm not makin' sense to you, but you'll see. Be true to yourself, to what's right, smile at the simple things, and don't let them get you all worked up about nothin'. Only get worked up for what matters. And when you see what matters, what's right, do it. They'll try to stop you 'cause people are scared of someone who's like that, who is clean, 'cause it makes them feel dirty by comparison; it makes them know they've given up, deep down where it hurts, and it pisses 'em off. That's why they take delight in the failure of others. I think this is why they love seeing a celebrity become a shooting star in another Hollywood scandal. But, and here's the important stuff, whether you make it or not, if you do what's right as you see it you'll always feel complete, 'cause you'll be completely you."

My throwaway cell phone buzzed.

"Where are you?"

"Hi, Senator. Yes, I'm here."

I started to leave, stopped, looked down into the wise man's eyes. I reached in my pocket and handed the homeless man the last of my cash. $422.

"Keep it," I said. "Whatever happens to me tonight, money won't matter either way."

The old man laughed. "Be good, young man, be good, and keep that positive attitude. That's the truest statement I heard in years."

23

IN THE THROES OF YOU

SENATOR HARRIS WASN'T the type who waits. He carried his fat frame along on his remarkable drive. As parts of him bounced, even jittered, his legs churned along with a wide, deliberate gait. I widened my stride to catch up, to keep pace as we went under the cement awnings of the Garden.

People felt the vibrations of Harris's footsteps, of his will, then saw his scowl and moved out of his overbearing way. His size and demeanor gave him his magnetism. It was what kept him in office for twenty-two years. He was a born leader. Bereft of wit, he filled the void with bearish bravado. He habitually chewed on unlit cigars. He hadn't lit one since his first heart attack, five years before. But he wouldn't know himself without one always ready to be chomped by his elephant-sized molars.

Senator Harris slammed his catcher's mitt hand into my chest, nearly sending me over backwards, as he declared, "Here, take this. It's Joshua's, oh, one of my aid's IDs. He looks enough like you now that you cut your hair as I told you to. Good to see you can take orders. Maybe there's hope for you yet."

"Yes, thank you, Senator, you won't regret this," I said as I memorized the name and address on the ID.

We strode through the Garden to waiting security.

"I'm sticking my fat neck out for you."

"You're not only doing the right thing, but you'll be the hero of the people for doing so, sir."

The senator flared his political smile, causing his cheeks to fatten into jowls. He clearly liked the idea of being the hero. Maybe he'd seem more presidential. He said, "I move well for a fat man, huh? It's all the underground tunnels between the Capitol Building and the congressional offices. I must walk ten miles a day and I don't have time to dillydally."

The security line snaked back and forth between velvet ropes for a hopeless stretch. The seats in the upper levels of the Garden were free, first-come-first-serve. Before the debate a half-dozen comedians were to take the stage. Then each party had two speakers to fire up the partisans before the live TV face-off at 8:00 p.m. The debate was being promoted with posters and television commercials more fitting of a UFC fight. On the posters the two candidates faced each other with grim expressions under the banner "Political Fight Night at the Garden." There hadn't been a debate like this since television made politicians looks more important than their messages, their sound bites more alluring than their policies, their smiling faces more believable than their dirty records.

"Follow me," ordered the senator as he strode away.

I fell into the politician's ample wake as we pushed through the crowd to a VIP line. I felt like a fool then. I'd have been better off hiding in the melee of street people piling in than following a senator up the aristocratic line.

Senator Harris looked at the men in dark suits—FBI, NSA . . .—and scoffed at me, "Hurry up, I'm late. Joshua, hurry along damn you, where's your ID?"

I saw the facial-recognition cameras and turned away from them as I said, "I've got it, Senator, and we're not that late yet. Don't worry." I placed my computer bag on a scanning belt.

"Don't worry? You dimwit!" said the senator as we walked through full-body scanners and then a metal detector.

I scooped my laptop bag from a scanner belt and heard someone try to ask something but was cut off by the senator declaring, "Move it, Joshua, damn you. Why didn't I take Michael? He's faster than this. You want to stay on my staff, you better move."

Two security guards looked at each other as they shook their heads and let me and the senator march away down a corridor and onto the main floor of the arena.

Senator Harris pushed a ticket into my hand. "We have seats in section two, right on the floor and in front. You're welcome to sit there. I'll be seen there after my speech. I don't know exactly what you're gonna do, but you'd better do it and do it right. I'll have your head if you fuck this up. I'm risking my career on you."

"I'll follow you backstage, sir. And then, after about two minutes, order me to go and find you a good cup of coffee and I'll, well, I'll find your revenge, sir."

"You don't sound as cocky now! Shit, all right. Get it done. That son of a bitch destroyed my health and my savings. He even included my waist size and my penchant for briefs over boxers in that damn profile. A lot of it wasn't even right. Some of my staffers had surfed on my computer and their tastes for Asian porn and Crate & Barrel crap was included in my likes file."

Backstage at Madison Square Garden before a show of this size was as much of a zoo as I hoped. Makeup artists, assistants, hangers-on, and celebrities were moving with the seemingly random business of bees in a hive. People in ones and twos shuffled around lit mirrors and makeup tables and others shouted into cell phones and politicians and celebrities paced as adrenaline fueled nerves. All the while security was trying to keep track, but couldn't.

Outside the stage lights had come on and the audience, now half in, began to murmur excitedly as red, blue, and white spotlights shot from the stage to the dome ceiling and spun and flashed as dry ice added smoke, drama. The cameras hadn't started rolling, but the B acts had begun. A political comedian was on the stage saying, "Welcome one and all to the greatest show on Earth, we have every make and size of creature here, Democrats, Republicans, and you, the v-o-t-e-r-s, maybe a few of you are even swingers, uh, I mean, swing voters, those indecisive souls with no real convictions. Whatever your affiliation or creed, now you're in the big top where some will guess your weight, for a fee, and others will offer elephant rides, and still more, you'll see, are asses, but don't be fooled, all are clowns, as soon you'll see. Why just now backstage a Republican congressman—can't recall his name, though he had big ears and a long, funny nose—asked me with fear in his big brown eyes, 'Have you seen the audience yet, I hear they're loaded for elephant.'"

"Boo," roared the audience and the comedian moved on through his lame skit.

"Tough audience tonight," gulped someone near me.

"Bloody rabble from the streets," said another.

With the acts begun the attention of everyone backstage projected out to the stage as others nervously prepared to step out in front of 20,000 impatient New Yorkers.

I spotted Secret Service agents here and there, but ignored them. They were looking for mad gunmen, terrorists, and such nutcases; they weren't after the man on the front pages. I used my peripheral vision to scan for FBI agents I'd met, especially Special Agents Rooney and Bent. Some in the room could have been FBI, especially one stiff-looking fellow in a corner. But I didn't see anyone I knew.

As Senator Harris berated a stylist for getting powder in his eyes, I noticed hallways leading to more private green rooms. I wondered if Verity was behind one of those doors preparing to unleash his so-called truth. The notion gave me a chill. I knew other doors would also, by now, hold the two presidential candidates. Then I noticed Secret Service agents guarding one corridor, and it was clear where they were.

I saw a production worker open a door and go into another hall. I concentrated on that doorway. There was a Garden security guard blocking access. I counted and thought that the blueprints I'd seen indicated that door led to the main and secondary production rooms up and down stairs. If I could get to the production room, I could be sure the files I'd replaced were still in place. I was worried their intrusion-detection software might have alerted them, even though I'd been careful to hide my tracks by digitally stepping in theirs.

"Joshua, make yourself useful. Get me a good cup of coffee. Move."

I nodded, moved fast, and had to turn my shoulders this way and that as I navigated makeup tables and people preparing to go out into the spotlight.

I peered down the hallways shooting off to private dressing rooms into the staging area of the Garden. These cinderblock halls were lined with posters from countless bands and hockey and basketball games and boxing matches from more than a century of New York theater. I knew the main production room was upstairs. It had a view of the floor from the south side. But I didn't need to get in there. I needed to get to the production room where promos would be built and audio cut and fed in as necessary. The live feed along with the pre-built commercials and pre-taped segments would then be streamed to satellites and over cable lines worldwide.

With all this security, some private, some federal, a lot of NY PD, and the Garden's staff, I had to be careful not to look like I was wandering. I moved deliberately but slowly across the rooms to the Garden security guard positioned in front of the maintenance corridor. The guard was a black woman with sharp, knowing eyes that could see a lie in the smile of a priest.

I smiled at her anyway, showed my ID, and said in an over-the-top, friendly way everyday New Yorkers find quant, "Ma'am, my name is Joshua Tompkins, I'm a special assistant to Senator Harris, one of your speakers tonight. He was wondering if I could speak to your head of production, or at least to someone on his or her staff. You see, the last time he spoke at one of these things they messed up his audio and announced him as 'Senator Horace.' Very sorry, but he's a pushy fellow and he just threatened to fire me . . . if, well, if you could just let me talk to someone on the production staff."

I sounded as pitiful as I could. I hoped this act might fool her into thinking I was just an insecure, nervous wimp trembling from the senator's wrath.

She looked right through me as her eyelids tightened as a cat's do just before pouncing. She cursed under her breath. She thought I was another pathetic, limp-wristed white boy, another metrosexual dandy. She pulled the ID out of my hand, rubbed it with her thumb. Hit it with a black light. Shook her head. Gave in. Pulled her radio off her belt, said, "Some senator's little helper is down here wantin' to talk to production. He looks impotent."

"Yeah, yeah, send him up," came a crackling reply, "but I don't have time for much."

She stepped aside and I found myself alone in a long, unfinished hall.

"Take the second elevator up. They'll buzz you in."

The door slammed shut behind.

I walked down the hall past framed posters of famous athletes and musicians. I could hear, feel the building humming above. I followed exposed electric lines, pipes. The ceiling panels were missing thanks to the upgrade in progress, but I didn't see the fiber-optic lines. I tried to picture the schematic of the building. I shook my head. Too many renovations over too many years, this place was unfathomable.

I hit the elevator button. Saw it was coming down. The door opened and I locked eyes with a young man in an argyle sweater and jeans. This guy had two days of growth on his young face and his hair was short and combed forward and shiny with hair gel. But all that was common enough; it was the way the man stared at me that had alarm bells ringing.

The man stopped the elevator door with his hand and said, "Hey, it's you."

"I can't deny that, it is indeed me."

"What the fuck are you doing?"

"Going up to production."

"The hell you are."

A hint of recognition exploded in me.

"Yeah it's me, or you, or the one who was you," said the man who had impersonated me.

"But you said you were an actor or . . . ?"

"Aren't you stupid. I don't know why we even tried to recruit you."

He pushed me across the hall. I lowered my shoulders and drove him back into the elevator.

He slammed an elbow into my ribs as we grappled.

The doors closed.

He got a finger into my right eye, knocking off my glasses. I fell back.

"You're supposed to be out there," said the man who was once me.

He hit the button to open the elevator door and pushed me back out. He kicked my glasses into the hall and said, "You better not come back in here."

I wanted to go in swinging—I'd beaten him once before—but then I'd likely get arrested. I forced myself to calm down. I picked up and put back on my glasses and tried to walk nonchalantly back out. I needed time to think.

"What happened to you?" asked the savvy security guard as I came back out.

"Oh, just tired, ma'am."

"Production kick your ass or somethin'?"

I was away and walking toward Senator Harris, who was standing, waiting, just seconds from taking the stage.

"I'll see you out in our seats, sir."

Senator Harris slowly ran his eyes up and down me, grinned and said, "Looks like you've been up to something."

Before I could tell him we'd have to bank on plan A an assertive voice declared, "Senator."

Senator Harris and I turned around to find the host of the night, Oliver Wissel, glaring with a hand outstretched to the senator.

"Oh, hi Oliver," said Senator Harris as the ends of his mouth drooped to a clown's exaggerated frown. Harris ignored the outstretched hand as he said, "I don't know how you pulled all this off, Wissel, but it looks like real political theater tonight."

Wissel smiled even wider and said, "Yes, Senator, real theater."

Wissel moved his brown eyes up and over me and took my hand with his still outstretched hand as he asked, "You all right?"

I still didn't have control of myself, but Senator Harris casually said, "Oh, this is my assistant, Joshua. He's always a little, uh, like this."

Wissel held my hand, looked deep into my eyes, and said with a subdued, penetrating tone and a tightening grip, "Yes, of course, good to see you made it, you're in for more than you bargained for tonight."

I thought that true but couldn't get a syllable out before Wissel was off introducing himself to someone else.

Then Harris was being ushered toward the stage and I traipsed out of the backstage area, and through security. I winced when I spotted Special Agent Bent staring at every face coming into the backstage area. I kept walking and was soon within the audience that was still taking seats with just minutes to go before the main show.

An usher pointed out a first-row seat.

I hesitated, then sat down, feeling exposed, like I was suddenly naked in a crowded room. There was no one to hide behind. I slouched down and hoped my meager disguise was enough.

A comedian was feet away from me on the stage joking, "This is a Spartan's dream debate all right, all we need is a pit to push the loser in. Now sure, you know Sun Tzu would be all for this battle; in *The Art of War* he tells us the greatest victory is won without fighting, but I say screw that, let's get Spartan tonight, let them debate, but then give them shields and see who has the mettle to shove the other off the battlefield in this arena. Now I know old Hamilton died in a duel just the other side of the Hudson River from here, but that's no fun, too quick."

The Garden was at capacity, all seated, all exuberant. Red, white, and blue spotlights ranged back and forth behind the comedian as he walked back to the curtain and hoisted two cardboard shields rented from a costume company. "You see, I've come with more than words tonight. What d'ya say? Fight, fight, fight . . ."

The audience picked up the chant and the comedian wouldn't leave the stage even as Senator Harris came lumbering out.

The comedian handed Senator Harris a shield. Took a combative posture. Harris was laughing, trying not to play the fool. When the comedian feinted, Harris, who had 150 pounds on him, shoved hard, sending the joker tumbling. The audience jumped to their feet. Then, as the comedian stood, bowed, and left, Harris said into the microphone, "Don't mess with an elephant. This is an historic night. This is a battle of right and wrong . . ."

Harris shifted into partisan politics. I still felt naked in the front row. The cameras were sure to pan over me again and again. Someone, if not the authorities, then some guy out there on the net or with a newspaper in his lap, was sure to see through my stupid facade. What should I do about that Truth Seeker I'd fought? They were in production. They controlled the show. Should I give myself up to tell the authorities? Maybe it wouldn't matter.

I'd replaced production files and had set e-bombs. As long they weren't found, I could be victorious, behind bars or free. I'd have to wait, but didn't feel comfortable just waiting. I didn't like that the Truth Seeker I'd fought wasn't surprised I was in the building, just that I was in the elevator going to production. What did that mean? I'd wanted to get into the production room to be sure my work had not been undone, but a Truth Seeker was already there. If they'd found all the files I'd replaced . . . well, I just might have to do something crazy.

Senator Harris wrapped up his five-minute speech with the declaration "forget the rhetoric you'll hear tonight, vote on their records," and then stomped down off the stage and plummeted into the seat next to me.

As another politician took their five-minute allotment, Harris leaned over and demanded, "What's going to happen here?"

"If all goes well, Verity will be publicly exposed. He won't be able to handle judgment from his looks, as I don't think he's even seen his own reflection in years."

"No shit?"

"Yeah, unless my hacking was discovered."

"Shit."

"Yeah, shit."

"When will we know?"

"Halfway through."

"A fucking lifetime. Why so long?"

"If I profiled him right off no one would get what was going on, there wouldn't be context for it, as a result he might skate. The audience needs time to settle in first. And anyway, I didn't want the changes I made found. They're buried and have the same names the files I replaced had. I even altered the metadata to—"

"Okay, shut up."

Oliver Wissel strutted onto the stage. Spotlights moved behind him drawing an American flag all the way to the ceiling of the arena. "Hail to the Chief" began to rock Madison Square Garden played by an unseen, though rocking brass band backed up by electric guitars.

After a rollicking minute the music fell away and the flag faded out. Behind Wissel was suddenly a digital screen two hundred feet high and three hundred feet wide. Wissel's live image appeared there over a moving background of politicians and flags and babies being kissed.

After a short, dramatic pause, the arena went silent and Wissel began, "This is no ordinary debate; it's a technological wonder as never before. Behind me is an interactive screen. It'll change as the candidates for the nation's top office speak. Watch it. It's preprogrammed with government data, polls, and quotes that'll be loaded thanks to voice-recognition software and their talking points. It'll keep track of their honesty and show the true, unbiased facts behind their assertions in real time. It's also linked to you at home and here. When you see text-message addresses you can email your views to live polls that will show if you like their points and agree with their policy positions. That's the basics of what will happen over the next ninety minutes, but there'll be a lot of surprises too. Get ready for a debate like no other.

"All the questions were written by me or chosen from your thousands of suggestions by me. Each candidate will have one minute to respond. They'll see a clock ticking on their lectern. When their minute is up their microphone will automatically shut off—no exceptions, nor extra time.

"So come on out and meet your voters," said Wissel and the two candidates walked out into the spotlights before the roaring crowd and all the glass eyes of the staring TV cameras. As they walked their practiced strides they seemed excited, though as perplexed as people who'd just been randomly selected by a televangelist and so really didn't know what they were in for.

They stopped uncomfortably behind lecterns twenty feet apart. They stood angled slightly toward Wissel, who was strutting without a lectern, free as a game-show host between them and the audience.

Behind the candidates rose live images of the candidates like color shadows growing from their feet and projected up by dramatic light cast from cameras just in front and below.

Wissel's live image faded from the huge screen. Between the living images of the candidates grew video of them campaigning at hospitals, of people in wheelchairs, of doctors with blood on their hands, of medical bills piling up all in a moving, changing montage.

Wissel faced the screen and the candidates, with his back to the audience, and bowed his head. He didn't even have a cue card or a teleprompter. Ten seconds, an eternity on air, passed before he slowly raised his face. Then something in the blankness of his eyes, a deadness in his expression, the seriousness of a cold-blooded killer in his face, frightened the two candidates. They thought to run but were held by the cameras and the clamoring 20,000.

Wissel turned left, asked, "My dear Democratic candidate, you were a district attorney in the state of New Jersey, but switched to defense and represented large pharmaceuticals in medical malpractice cases. Those companies later donated $750,000 to your first congressional campaign. In a phone call in 1999 to your largest donor you said . . ."

Wissel stopped talking and speakers all over the arena played the candidate's voice saying, "Yes, I'll work to appropriate funds for your research. This is critical, I get that. Just give me time. I have some favors to do, some bargains to make. I know I owe you."

Wissel looked deeply at the Democratic nominee and asked as a parent might a child who stole another's candy, "Was that ethical?"

She began to stammer, "Where did you get . . . you see . . . I . . . you know . . . the research they were conducting was for the greater good."

Wissel interrupted her: "It was inadvertently recorded in a federal wiretap. They didn't intend that it be aired, but it's in the public domain. It was provided by the same online profiler who exposed Mayor Bill Perkins. Voice-recognition software verified it to be authentic. What was the research for?"

She was flustered, a very unusual state for a woman who'd earned the nickname "the Executioner" from her allies, and yet more graphic things by her enemies, and so she rambled, "Well, I don't recall. We passed a lot of, you know, bills for . . . maybe it was for the testing of that liver drug, uh, Exalter, yes, I think, I mean, that could be it. I was just doing what was right for the greater good. They contribute to a lot of politicians. They're an important medical research company."

When her minute was gone, Wissel turned to the Republican nominee. "Senator, you were a doctor in a family practice. You were sued for malpractice thirty-four times. You lost or settled twelve times. You left your practice with a rating below the national average. You once told a medical review board . . ."

Again Wissel stopped and the speakers in the arena took over: "I don't deserve this. Complications happen. That child lived. I did all I could. That mother was using narcotics. There were reactions. She wasn't honest with us. I didn't know. That mother, if there was justice, would be behind bars. She's negligent, yet she sued me. I only settled because the legal bills were mounting and she is a well, attractive, a believable type person. She doesn't have a record. I didn't have a case."

The Republican senator was squirming. A photo of the mother, a beautiful woman holding the hand of her brain-damaged child, was two hundred feet tall. Some people were booing, others crying.

The Republican nominee began to explain, "Uh, that was supposed to be a closed review. I don't know how you got that audio. You can't blame me. That's why we need tort reform in this country. I had no recourse. It's expensive for doctors to practice in this litigious society. If a mechanic troubleshoots a problem on an auto as best he can, he doesn't get sued. When a doctor uses the best science to make the best diagnosis possible, he gets sued if he or she errs."

Some in the audience were hissing, a few shouting derogatory slurs. A few spectators threw empty cups at the stage. Security began searching for them.

The Republican sweated for his minute before his mic shut off, then he breathed like a sprinter after a race.

Wissel stood with his posture too perfect, too easy for the likes of the candidates, as he asked, "Senator and Congresswoman, there is a solution here. Wouldn't you both agree that we not only need digital, searchable medical records, but that also access to them by the courts and medical personnel must be mandated and also available to patients? If you are both right, wouldn't the truth about these people's medical records and your behind-the-scenes support for research set you free? After all, it's easy for me in the context of this forum to make these things sound wrong. But if all the truth were available you could defend yourself honorably, or pay for your actions truly. So with that in mind, Congresswoman, would you support medical reform to open and standardize medical records and research?"

She squeezed the sides of her lectern until her knuckles turned white as she smiled pleasantly and said, "Of course, within reason. We must have honest accountability . . ."

When she finished her minute, Wissel asked the Republican candidate, "Do you concur, Senator? And if so, would you say that, as a Republican and former practicing physician, we can't simply trust the state and the state alone with these records?"

"Yes, given the right privacy controls, private doctors with their patients' permission . . ."

Wissel smiled like he was nearing checkmate and didn't care if his opponent knew the trap was set. When the Republican's minute ended, he asked, "So then, you both agree medical records must go digital and be as available as each individual wants; you seem to only disagree, though unsurely, with how much the state should be involved. So let me try to help you along. Should those who're receiving state care via Medicaid, Medicare, or some other taxpayer-funded program have their files watched by the government while those who don't retain the ability to remain private? After all, doing so would make our Medicaid programs and prescription-drug benefit programs and so on more proficient; for example, if we had updated, digital records, we could know if a person receiving taxpayer-funded care is getting the best medical help, or if they're abusing the system. The system could then be tailored nationally to best benefit the individual, isn't that right, Congresswoman?"

"Yes," she said, "I've actually said something like that before—"

Her mic went dead as Wissel interrupted, "Yes you have, and as a district attorney, you often used medical records against defendants."

"Yes," she said, pissed that he could so casually cut off her mic whenever he chose. That wasn't in the debate contract. Then she reddened from rage when a recording of a closing statement she made in court, a court that didn't allow tape recorders or video cameras, aired over the arena and into millions of homes: "Sarah Johnson is not who she seems. She's on fourteen different drugs, three of them illegal, according to her blood work. She's a druggie. She's medicated right now. She's sick. She's an addict. She did commit domestic violence as a result of her illness. She needs help, not her children back. Why she's not even here right now, not really. She's in Neverland floating on a happy cloud of uppers."

The tape stopped and the Democratic candidate seethed, "Wait a second," but her microphone was dead. So she yelled, "That's not true," just as her mic came back on, making her seem desperate, angry, mean. She tried to rally by dousing her anger with outrage: "This is not fair. How dare you. Justice was served in that case, thanks to me."

"Was it?" asked Wissel as a photo of the woman walking out of court with her four-year-old daughter lovingly in her arms appeared on the screen. "Your decision was overturned when it was found her identity had been stolen and someone had used her credit cards to buy all sorts of prescriptions."

"I didn't know."

Wissel turned back to the Republican. "I haven't forgotten about you, Senator. Didn't you, in 2002, vote for the Health Information Portability and Accountability Act, an act that makes those privacy notices people sign in doctors' offices give patients little control over their personal data? And isn't it true that those forms merely describe how the data will be used and disclosed and that the government is now in control of peoples' private medical data?"

The senator began stumbling over his own tongue as he managed to say, "I wouldn't characterize it that, I, uh . . ."

After his minute ended Wissel asked, "You're spinning like a top, Senator. But I think people see the truth in your eyes, so let me move on: Isn't it true that when you closed your private practice you were investigated for missing drugs and odd prescription authorizations?"

"My intern was investigated for selling some things on some internet site, but—" His mic went dead.

"But you were never cleared?"

His mic came back on. "The investigation is still open, but I was never under suspicion."

It went off again.

A sheriff's dour expression filled the huge screen, the speakers picked up the officer's voice from a 1998 press conference: "We currently don't know who's telling the truth and therefore who's responsible. But this is a murder case and therefore will stay open. An elderly man OD'd on a lethal mix, a possible suicide. We know the drugs came from this doctor's office, but can't say who sold them. It's a he said, she said case."

The Republican candidate had answered that allegation before, so he regurgitated his prepared response: "As I've testified, my prescription pad was stolen, as were some drug samples from my office. There are police reports."

Wissel said, "Time for a commercial break."

Wissel turned to the cameras for the first time since the beginning and said, "We have more surprises in store. Don't go away."

As the candidates tried to walk calmly back behind the curtain to meet their staffs where they'd blow their tops, I nearly fell from my front-row seat as my head spun with a startling possibility.

A comedian came on to entertain the audience as viewers back home watched commercials. Meanwhile, I turned my attention to Wissel, who was lingering at the edge of the stage, still in the public's protective eye. Wissel merely picked up a tall glass of water and sipped from it casually. I stared a long time at him. I watched the man's eyes, tried to see into them. He was too far away to see clearly, but there was something about them.

I opened my laptop. Set it on my knees. Turned it on. My hands were shaking.

The comedian tried to keep the Garden's audience entertained: "Now is this political theater or what? While the candidates were being grilled their staffs were backstage squaring off with ballpoint pens like a bunch of Crips and Bloods armed with shivs." But the 20,000 weren't listening to the jester on stage, they were gossiping about what might come next. This was all so extraordinary.

The reporters and pundits were speaking excitedly to cameras, all enthralled, all amazed. There had never been a debate like this. No settled-on questions, no allowance for spin . . . a screen behind ready to play gotcha moments at any time.

My computer fired up.

"What's going on here? Have you failed?" said Senator Harris.

I ignored him. I opened the MIT program that would compare writing styles, thought processes. I soon found transcripts of Wissel's dialogue on his cable network's site. I copied and pasted transcripts from shows into the program and compared them to Verity's word choices.

The senator banged me with his elbow and said, "What's going on?"

I ran the program.

The senator hit me harder.

A ninety percent match. Verity is either Wissel or they're brothers.

"Sidney!"

Or maybe Wissel is just reciting verbatim what Verity sent him, maybe this is a condition, sell your soul and you get . . . ah hell, it's a chance I'll have to take.

"Sidney!"

I shook my head, answered, "Another segment and we'll know."

I was stalling, trying to think.

Wissel was on again, smiling, boasting in the center of the stage: "Hello, America. We're just starting to get somewhere. Thanks for your text messages. You can see them reflected in the interactive polls. So far you don't prefer either of these two, but we'll see. A lot more is in store tonight."

Wissel turned back around to face the two candidates.

"Now Senator, you cosponsored the Online Crime Act, a bill designed to nail online pedophiles. The legislation made it easier for authorities to track, to listen in on, and thereby nab child pornographers. It also inadvertently resulted in convictions for offenses from public exposure to murder. You've empowered Big Brother, albeit to spy on a politically unfavorable subgroup. So then, do you think this act should be expanded so we can catch other criminals online? For example, to track, say, all sales of stolen goods on eBay?"

The Republican candidate shrugged, said, "Not necessarily. That's a little too broad for my liking. We must be careful about extending the powers of government . . ."

When his minute ended, Wissel asked, "So some criminals have more rights than others?"

"Well, no. Some are just more of a public danger than others."

"But isn't it true that repeat offenders don't stop with pedophiles, that, in fact, rapists and muggers repeat their crimes statistically more often than pedophiles?"

"That may be so, I'm not sure, but when children are involved . . ."

Wissel, nodded, said, "Ah, I see, you're making a moral distinction to especially protect children. Well then, how about your record? You lost in court five times for malpractice. Two of those cases involved children, so let's see."

The screen behind showed the blurred-out faces of two children as emails scrolled up the screen. Then it stopped on a highlighted section that Wissel read aloud: "'No one is perfect. I didn't mean to prescribe . . . [bleep] happens . . . can we make this go away? I have a political future to think of.'"

"So Senator," asked Wissel, "that's your email and by your own rules it should be public, so no complaints, please."

"How did you? That's not the same thing at all. How did you . . . ?"

"That same anonymous source," said Wissel. "Wouldn't it be better if we could just do away with those nasty anonymous types on the internet who feel so empowered cloaked in pseudonyms; especially this rogue, Verity, the truth teller who's nailed so many in the political class this season?"

But Wissel didn't let the Republican nominee respond; instead he turned to the Democratic candidate and asked, "Congresswoman, you voted for legislation to give drug companies the freedom to use patient data to better market their products. Why?"

She said, "We want people who need help to know about the most recent developments and scientific breakthroughs . . ."

After her minute, Wissel asked, "Isn't part of the reason because of campaign contributions?"

"No, I—" Her mic went off.

Votes positioned alongside donations streamed up the huge screen and the audience grumbled. Then a picture with the words "pharmaceutical lobbyist" under it appeared. A crackling voice recorded over a phone line echoed around the arena, "Don't worry, we'll make the donations come from subsidiaries so OpenSecrets. com won't burn you, Congresswoman. No problem. This is all for the greater good, so please don't worry."

The 20,000 around the arena began to bellow, "Boo."

Wissel raised his hands in the air and turned to the crowd as he declared, "I could condemn every member of Congress as easily. And perhaps it's time we did. Enough of the backroom dealings that are out of sight of the American public. Enough of journalists rooting for their team. It's time for retribution. It's time for honesty."

Both candidates looked at each other, then to the restless audience. The two-hundred-foot screen began to scroll Congress members' backroom dealings, data showing political donations aligned with votes.

Wissel said, "My network assembled this new database. Just type in your candidate's name or district and you'll see everything. And not just what they declared. But also where online contributions—something some have been sneaky enough to hide—originated from; I'm talking real names this time, not Sponge Bob, E-Queen, or some other Web pseudonym that candidates are now letting, or encouraging, people to hide behind. Campaign finance laws, after all, were written by lawyers; they're outdated legal trash. Here's the truth."

I said aloud, "But I replaced those files."

Senator Harris began tossing his bulbous head side to side.

The audience looked puzzled. They needed a sound bite to rally behind.

"America," said Wissel as the crowd sat befuddled, "I give you your congressmen's real motivations: money, which equals power. Maybe this is overload. No matter. Make sure your local news outlets help. Digest it. All this is now being posted on our network's website. But don't blame the politicians too much, as they're simply lost in this dirty system, trying to compete according to outdated, complex rules in an age of partisan gaming. So really, isn't it the system that's to blame? Don't we need to reform the system? After all, as you'll find, many in Congress are good, honorable men and women, it's just they're caught in a dirty system that rewards deceit."

The files I'd changed weren't there. I fret as each second punched me in the gut.

Senator Harris started to get his weight up and moving.

I grabbed his arm as I begged, "Another segment, sir, another segment, please. I have to think."

I wasn't sure if I should just give the government everything I had. If I should point to Wissel and scream "Verity." I didn't think doing so would free myself and Aster—even if they believed me, even if I were right—as they'd want to keep as much leverage on me as possible. They'd repress the image of Verity. They'd want Verity's virus for themselves. They'd classify and patent it under the NSA's ability to secretly patent such technology. Big Brother would win. Everything would remain in the shadows.

The senator fell heavily back into his seat. He was sweating from the exertion of terrible wrath. His profile had been let out by Verity already; as a result, he'd found a person's profile didn't necessarily lead to more honesty, but rather to more spin; that's why he went along with me, why he helped me. He began to worry that he'd let his lust for revenge lure him to his own destruction. He was harboring a wanted man. He began to wring his big, fat hands.

Both candidates turned around to watch the screen. The audience was confused, but riveted. There was too much to digest. The press hadn't tied it together into sound bites. They didn't understand the narrative. The government, until this moment, had kept control, had kept Verity's existence uncertain, mostly unknown to the public. They didn't get all these allusions to the online profiler. Most journalists had simply taken credit for the Deep Throat sort of information they'd gotten. The audience was searching for what to believe.

Wissel seemed too confident. Clearly he was leading them somewhere, to some deeper conclusion. He said, "Congresswoman, the next question is yours."

She gave Wissel the sharp glare of condemnation she used to save for her opposing counsel's witnesses.

The audience settled down.

Wissel asked, "What crimes should constitute a person's loss of privacy? You voted to pass the Combined DNA Index System, or CODIS, to keep track of violent criminals and sexual predators. Then you voted for the Justice for All Act to expand the system to include samples from all newly convicted federal felons, including drug offenders and white-collar criminals. Many states now use this DNA system to get samples from everyone they arrest, whether they're convicted or not. So is this right? Should anyone arrested have their DNA taken and then be tracked and treated as the usual suspects, even if they're never convicted?"

The audience started to breathe again. While Wissel spoke, the question "Should all felons lose their privacy?" popped up on the screen. People began text messaging answers. Ninety percent of the rabble thought "yes."

The Democratic nominee answered, "All violent criminals, I think, should have their DNA taken and lose their privacy. For the sake of society, the government should track them and watch them for specified periods. We do that with parole now, but I think we could do so more effectively with GPS tracking, online surveillance, and . . ."

She completed her minute and Wissel said, "The government only? There is now a law on the books that allows people to find out if a pedophile has moved into their neighborhood. Can't we do the same with other crimes?"

"Well, I, for the people's own good, the government is there to protect them. I'd worry about vigilantism. The state can handle tracking these perps."

"You want the state, with no transparency, to have the power to watch all the citizens they deem to be threats?"

She shook her head. "No. The Privacy Act of 1974, and its subsequent amendments, outlaw the keeping of records on Americans in most cases; however, as a prosecutor I found the state does need to watch some felons. I think law enforcement should move into the twenty-first century. Online tactics, computer forensics, high-tech security with digitized biometrics, security cameras on street corners, and more need to be paid for so we can safeguard everyone. England has done a great job with facial recognition on security cameras positioned all around London. We need to watch for crimes for our own good."

Wissel turned to the Republican candidate. "Senator, does the state need the ability to watch the populace? Or is there a better way?"

The Republican said, "The Electronic Communications Privacy Act, the Privacy Act, even the FISA law are all designed to be checks on government surveillance."

"Do they now?" asked Wissel rhetorically. "There are exceptions and loopholes in all those laws that allow the government, especially its divisions and contractors, to profile Americans, even to see what library books we read and where we're navigating online. So let me ask you this: What if the state didn't have a monopoly on the information? That wouldn't be Orwellian. Let me give you both an example."

Wissel turned to the audience seated in front and above in the upper decks and circling all around in the arena's seating. The lights dimmed. Then a spotlight found a person seated in section 127, to Wissel's left and above. Wissel said, "Rise, Tom Johansen. Time to publicly pay for your sins. You were caught on facial-recognition software coming in. We know you haven't paid your taxes in eight years."

Tom jumped up, began to step around people's legs to exit stage left as a spotlight followed him. People wouldn't move out of his way. They just stared at him with glares of condemnation.

The spotlight next found a person in the press corps. "Why hello, Jane Thompson. You illegally have a rent-controlled apartment, don't you? This city has financial woes and you, a reporter calling for a more progressive tax structure, aren't paying your share."

She saw reporters smiling at her, wagging their fingers.

Then a spotlight found a seat in the upper deck. "Why hello, Wayne Labrozzi. Aren't you wanted for rape?"

Labrozzi jumped up, began to run. Security wasn't sure if they should stop him. Dozens of other men and women got out of their seats and started to maneuver past others' knees as they kept their eyes down, away from all the judgmental glares.

Then the spotlight found a seat in the front row. "Why Sidney McDaniel, how did you get in here? You're wanted for treason, you little Judas."

24

CONDEMNED

THE SPOTLIGHT BURNED into me. I could feel the glares of millions. Their eyes were searching every part of me, looking into my eyes, over my nose, mouth, and ears. They were judging me. I couldn't even see back. The white spotlight was blinding, making me look away, making me look guilty as I looked down and shielded my face with my hands.

Something hit me in the back of the head. Curses hissed at me from far away and right behind me. The senator was stomping his feet. His hands were going white-knuckled grabbing his knees as he leaned over his legs and looked left into me.

After a pause, Verity said, "Sidney, your picture is on the front page of every paper in town. Come and get him, New York's finest. He has a story to tell. Someone to betray."

Then the spotlight left me to nab another and I was suddenly so cold. The hot light was gone, but I was still there waiting for judgment.

I thought to run, but knew sprinting through the packed arena would be foolhardy.

Meanwhile, Senator Harris's eyes were bulging as he shook with wrath.

As security moved in, I turned to the senator and asked, even begged: "Come with me, sir. We can still win. If you leave me now, we both lose!"

Hands pulled me out of my seat and a half-dozen security guards, led by Special Agent Bent, moved me along side aisles past staring thousands to a private room in the back and up.

I looked back once and saw Senator Harris following, his big legs motoring his fat torso along.

As hands gripped, bruised my triceps, I tried to make a new plan. The FBI agents moved me along roughly. They wanted me to know they controlled me, that escape was impossible. Their steel-toed dress shoes kicked my legs as we went up stairs and their elbows slammed my ribs as we turned corners.

Far behind I heard Wissel saying, "I've spotlighted a dozen criminals here. I could go on all night. Few are truly innocent. My point is we should be careful with casting the first stone. But there are obviously issues with the system that condones, even rewards, this kind of behavior. So the system needs to be opened up.

"So Congresswoman, tell me . . ."

I was pushed into a small room, a dark office lit only by a window looking out onto the floor. A swivel chair slammed into the backs of my knees. I fell into the chair. A door slammed shut behind.

A ruckus exploded in the hallway as Senator Harris demanded to be allowed in.

Meanwhile, a half-dozen people stood around me in dark suits like menacing shadows in an almost dark bedroom.

A cigar flared in a corner. Its red glow exposed Special Agent Bill Rooney's roiled expression for a few seconds. Rooney growled, "Sidney, what the fuck are you doing here?"

Before I managed a reply, Rooney's billowing chest deflated as the door to the room burst open, washing in fluorescent light from a hall that was quickly blotted out by Senator Harris's ample frame.

"I'm Senator Harris. I demand to be in this room."

Rooney jumped to his feet while barking, "You have no business here, sir. Though we may be visiting you soon to find out why you helped this traitor get so close to the man or the woman who will be the next president of the United States."

"I'm on the—"

"Your position and committee status give you no authority here."

Agent Bent moved toward the door, said, "Sorry, Senator," as he began to push the large man from the doorway.

But I shouted, "Excuse me. I still have rights. Such as to an attorney being present. Senator Harris is my attorney."

The corners of Rooney's mouth plummeted to a frown.

Harris buffaloed Bent out of his way. "I'm still a licensed attorney. Mr. McDaniel has hired me. And, as you know, I have the proper security clearances."

Rooney demanded, "Are you licensed in New York?"

Harris parried, "This is a federal case, is it not?"

Rooney tried a different angle as his tone weakened: "Senator, attorney-client privilege won't save you from the laws you've broken."

"That's a question for a court to answer."

Rooney pulled Harris's assistant's ID out and threatened, "This is a felony."

Harris wasn't the type who rattled easily. He simply smiled as he said, "Prove it in court. But before we start all that legal warfare, why don't we deal with the crisis at hand. I think Sidney has enough to help you right now that'll benefit us all. But if you continue this blind attack he'll clam up and we'll see what happens in the courtroom and in the theater of public opinion."

As Harris spoke a realization smacked me. Aster had been making sure the profiling the Truth Seekers were doing was legal, or at least defendable in court. Then there was the Truth Seeker who didn't seem surprised I was in the building. And the fact that the breaks I'd gotten to get into Verity's hard drive had been easy. Verity had been getting ready for something. This was all planned. He was still following a script. Perhaps this was even why Verity had set the spotlight on me. Verity, whether he was Wissel or not, wanted to be nabbed, but at the proper time, which seemed to be after he does whatever it is he is planning to do during the debate. He wanted a public trial, maybe even to be nailed to a cross. It'd start his movement.

He even called me Judas.

I suddenly understood I had to do something unpredictable; I had to leapfrog ahead to foil the plot. So I bit my tongue and tried to think of the most outlandish thing I could do.

Rooney sat down and said, "Bent, close that door and turn on a light. This had better be good, Sidney, we don't have time for much."

Senator Harris flashed his politician smile as he asked, "What are you smoking? My doctor only lets me chew on them now."

"A Dominican, a Diamond Crown, robusto number two."

"Not bad. Even secondhand it tastes all right. Ah hell, give me one. Let's smoke as we work this out; there's no time for dillydallying."

I took a long, deep breath. Harris was an expert at deal making. He was used to the backroom Beltway compromise. Harris and Rooney eyed each other and obviously approved of what they saw. They were two old-school types right out of a Raymond Chandler novel. There weren't many of these dinosaurs left in public service. They could trust each other, as long as their interests ran parallel courses, which they seemed to be doing at this time. They were mature men who played by the same gentlemanly rules. They knew they weren't dealing with the urbane metrosexuals with law degrees and badges and no conception of honor, as so many men were these days.

"All right, Sidney," said Rooney, "talk and talk fast."

To bust free of that erroneous profile I said the boldest thing I could think of: "I need you to take me to the production room and to arrest everyone I point to, then I need you to let me take charge of the show."

"What?"

"There is no time to explain. I can give you Verity and his Truth Seekers, his disciples, right here, right now, but there is no time to explain. And we'll have to move in there quietly. If you're spotted taking me there there's no telling what will happen."

"I can't just—"

"You can and will. I can make you the hero who got the super criminal. But before I do I want a full pardon for myself and for Aster from the president of the United States."

"What the fuck? That's not possible."

I looked at Senator Harris, said, "The president is in your party and is one of your pals, Senator. You can call him. Just tell him what I showed you and make the pardons contingent on my success at taking down Verity."

Senator Harris chomped his cigar, nodded. "I can do that, but there is no way we can have pardons in hand in time."

"I'll take your word as my attorney, Senator."

Senator Harris took a long puff, leaned close, and whispered, "How did you know I was an attorney?"

"Aren't all of you politicians lawyer scum?"

Harris laughed hard as he stood and pulled out his phone. "Excuse me a minute, gentlemen."

Rooney began to pace, to shout orders. He didn't like giving control to this turncoat. But he could feel the moment moving out of his grasp and thought perhaps this was the only way.

Stopping the show wouldn't be winning but would fuel public outrage, speculated Rooney as he glanced to the stage at the sweating candidates. But this, this was so unpredictable.

The debate was only halfway through. The audience was quaking. Security was losing control of all the people who'd come in off the streets, of the bottom rung of society then becoming a mob in the upper levels. All the questions, all the data, seemed to be leading to some choreographed outcome, something Rooney must stop, but he didn't know what that might be.

"The president agrees, let's move," said Harris as the show outside went to commercial break.

A Madison Square Garden security guard jogged in front to lead the way. The senator walked behind and Rooney alternated power walking and jogging to keep up. An entourage of a half-dozen agents surrounded me and moved me along like Secret Service agents do a presidential motorcade.

25

BE BOLD

THE PRODUCTION ROOM'S door burst open and a half-dozen FBI agents flooded in, hands on firearms, voices blaring, "No one moves; no one speaks."

The dozen people inside stopped. No one spoke, just froze.

The production room was only thirty by forty feet and was filled with electronics. Servers blinked in corners, along walls. Red and blue fiber-optic cables ran from HD switchers and servers to soundboards. Flat screens showing camera angles were positioned in front. Four people sat at computer stations. Two had headsets. The production manager stopped pacing, ordering personnel to load promos and data, and stood wide-eyed. An electronic hum was the only sound still emanating.

In walked Special Agent Rooney. He was breathing like a horse after a race. He swept his puffy eyes across the dozen people in the small room. He pulled the cigar from his fat, gasping lips and blew blue smoke throughout the controlled climate and over the sensitive electronics.

Senator Harris and I moved in behind and Rooney broke the loaded pause by saying, "All right, Sidney, who do I arrest?"

I stepped around Rooney and settled my gaze on a twenty-something man with a headset, bruised face, and torn suit, on the man I'd fought. "Start with him. He's a Truth Seeker."

"Hey now, uh, wait a second," struggled the man as he went for his keyboard.

Bent grabbed the man's neck, tossed him down.

Rooney smiled, said, "Take him into the hall, Bent. Who else?"

"You, how long have you worked here?" I asked a middle-aged woman.

"Um, about nine years," she stammered.

"Who has worked here less than five?"

"Well, Harold, Beth . . ."

"Just point them out."

She hesitated.

"It's important."

She began pointing hesitantly at people who wilted as her index finger found them. Four more were taken from the room. The production manager stood baffled. He finally managed, "What, what is this all about?"

Rooney began to speak, but I spoke over him: "Just do your thing. I'll have questions for you later. First, how long until we're back live?"

The production manager pointed to a clock, said, "Ninety-three seconds and counting."

"Oliver Wissel's earpiece, whose voice is he listening to?"

"Someone from his own news team, up in their announcer's booth, uh, the main booth, overlooking the floor. His producer, she's the only one. It's what they wanted. This is just the production room, we're loading the files and sounds they've given us. It's all a little top secret, you know, because this is a presidential debate and they don't want either camp to know what the questions are in advance, so we haven't even seen the files, I mean—"

I raised a hand for him to stop, looked at Rooney.

"I'm on it," said Rooney and started to leave.

"Watch her, but don't do anything until I say."

Rooney turned his cigar-filled mouth to look over his left shoulder at me. "What, why . . . ?"

"Don't ask me questions. Just get close to her. Be ready to take her down. When you do it, and you won't until I call your cell, take her down fast while Wissel is speaking. We don't want her to be able to communicate that she's been apprehended. In fact, take them all down, all of the people in their booth and do it fast. We'll take over the controls from here."

I turned my attention to the production manager, asked, "We can do that, can't we?"

"Well yes," he said as his eyes searched my face. "I suppose it's technically possible. We've never done that before, but yes, we have the headsets and such in case of . . ."

Rooney's frown drooped his face as his eyes grew and his mouth grasped, "You're not saying?"

But I had moved on and simply said, "Okay, forty-two seconds. I want you all to go on as normal. I'll let you know when not to go on as normal. I want no unnecessary communications from this room to anyone outside."

Rooney bustled out with three agents. Two agents stood with postures as straight and still as mannequins in corners. Senator Harris headed for the green room. He wanted to be ready to preside.

The production manager began to rigidly direct a few people to different stations.

I pulled out my laptop. Plugged it into the main board, said, "Just calm down and do your thing. Oh, and make the necessary preparations to take control of the show."

"Yeah right," said the manager as he looked at the silent men in dark suits with their hands on firearms.

I found that the files I'd replaced hadn't been replaced after all. I guessed I'd been led into a pseudo-server. One set up as a decoy to mirror the database that had been really active. I'd been fooled with a sophisticated trap I'd used in the past to safely nab hackers. I felt like an amateur.

They'd been on to me all along; I'd been used. So then, why did they let me think I was getting away with hacking their system and replacing their files? It didn't make sense. They could have just stopped me. They could have even traced me, had me arrested. Why did they take the risk of letting me get so close?

I shook my head as I began replacing the files in the real database. No hacking needed, as I was on the inside this time. It was easier than before, as I knew where to go. But the next step was harder, as this was theater. I had to do this right. I'd only get one take. This was a live show. Millions were tuned in. I needed the right effects. No mistakes now. This wasn't hacking, which is a creative process of trial and error, this was showmanship. I had an idea and didn't allow myself to think that I might be miscalculating.

"We're live," said the production manager.

Wissel strutted back out behind his smile saying, "We're more than halfway through and are getting somewhere, an issue at a time. We have one more critical topic to cover before we show you something that will change, if not this race, then surely the political system we now find ourselves trapped in. Stay tuned, this is no normal debate, we're about to get to all the truth and nothing but the truth."

Wissel paused, turned his gaze to the lecterns and to the man and woman exposed behind them and asked, "Congresswoman, while out of power both parties have called for an end to anonymous earmarks, spending mandates attached to bills in the dark of night. Monies that lead to graft, to special-interest favors, to vote buying. You've also called for the abolition of the earmark, yet you have brought 134 earmarks back home to your constituents during the past twelve years."

Wissel stopped, pointed to the screen behind, said, "There they are."

The 20,000 all around, above, and below began to snicker, to hoot.

Wissel continued, "You've passed earmarks for muskrat research in New Jersey marshes, $800,000, beach cleaning for hypodermic needles, $1.2 million, to pay for global warming–alleviating gas nozzles, $24 million, and for street crime–seeing surveillance cameras, $6 million. Yet all those particular earmarks had no name attached. They were done anonymously. Why don't you want credit? And, shouldn't the people at least know who is spending their money?"

The Democratic candidate felt like she was back in the courtroom in one of those cases where even her star witness lied to her. She was a fighter. She could take a punch. She'd spent her career in New Jersey politics, not Iowa's school boards. So she said, "I am a reformer. But I have not yet been able to run the country, let alone my party. So I've worked as best I can in the system we have. We need more accountability, more transparency . . ."

She finished her minute smoothly and Wissel asked, "Didn't all of the groups that received the earmarks just mentioned give money to your campaigns?"

Her eyes rolled into her head as if to search out the facts as the cameras stared and her voice fluttered, "Well, I'm not sure, I—"

"Let me clarify your thinking, Congresswoman. Look at the screen behind you."

Lines of donations appeared alongside those four highlighted earmarks.

The audience hummed "Ooohhh."

The congresswoman clenched her teeth, began to speak but found her mic dead again and nearly marched across the stage with her fists churning.

Wissel ignored her death stare, turned to the Republican, and said, "Senator, as a conservative Republican I am surprised at your record on spending . . ."

I watched in real time as the files were being accessed from the server. They were in a choreographed sequence. This had all been practiced, which was why Wissel didn't need direction via his earpiece; he avoided that need perhaps because communications with producers could certainly be monitored by the NSA.

Next a video of the Republican senator calling earmarks "a vote-buying evil" was played juxtaposed beside his hundreds of earmarks.

Wissel asked, "No one in public office should be able to hide anonymous earmarks, dirty campaign cash, or special-interest pandering. Isn't that what's just and right?"

They both answered, "Yes."

I opened the next files in the sequence to be loaded and shown on the two-hundred-foot screen in the Garden and on TV screens all over the country and world.

I grabbed my cell phone, dialed, said, "Now, now, take them down now!"

"Ah, honesty," transitioned Wissel as he turned to the then standing 20,000 and addressed them directly: "Now we're going to see everything, to know all. It's time America makes a real, honest choice in this election. This digital age is backfiring on Big Brother. The people are again going to be in charge of their government, and I do mean their government. Here are your two candidates' profiles. All their dirty deeds, all their virtues, all their records from medical to criminal to voting records, everything. Here are the profiles of our two leading candidates, a man and a woman now in a dead heat. Who will you vote for? Read their profiles, not the spin from cable news pundits or newspaper op-ed writers. Read the facts of their lives and decide."

The two candidates blanched, spun.

Wissel pointed at the two-hundred-foot-high screen. Two photos appeared. One was of Verity, the one recorded from my laptop, the other was of Wissel.

"What's this?" blurted Wissel as the two photos moved on top of each other, then separated again before slowly moving together again. Under the photos, in huge red letters, were the names "Wissel" and "Verity."

The audience jumped to their feet, but were remarkably quiet. The photos were the same, except for small cosmetic changes; they were the same person.

The two candidates began smiling, turning, staring at Wissel.

Someone screamed, "Wissel is Verity."

A caricature appeared below the two photos of an ancient hairless man sitting on a stool with his back bent as a chimpanzee does when it squats. His skin was the color of a fish's belly. His fingers were long, as thin and pointed as talons. He was peering into a mirror, the reflection was of Oliver Wissel. In his right hand was a large stone, written on the stone was the word "privacy." Behind him were a dozen worshippers all bowing at his bony feet.

Facts from Verity's life, his truth, what he'd done to people, the identities of his disciples, the effects of his profiles and much more—everything I could dredge up from Verity's private computer and the system they'd just built—appeared and scrolled up the big screen.

Wissel stumbled toward the screen as if intoxicated while hollering wildly, "What, what's this?"

Verity turned to the audience, saw them laughing. They were amused. His caricature was drawing snickers, scoffs. He'd become a buffoon, a fool. His real face, the weary, wrinkled mess without even eyebrows over its egotistical eyes, fermented condemnation. People were judging him by his looks, sure in the fact that a person may be born with genetically determined looks, but that they also shape and distort the flesh according to who they are. In him they saw egotism, cynicism, mirth. Deep in his eyes—his eyes without colored contacts hiding their true color and thoughts—they saw shades of a man who disdains others, who even dislikes himself; they saw a sick, twisted, power-hungry man.

"No, no that's not me," he shrieked, but found his microphone had been shut off.

The candidates began to laugh. As they did they realized their mics were back on.

The congresswoman was fastest on her feet. She asked in a tone she once reserved for combative witnesses: "So Oliver Wissel, aka Verity, who is the true charlatan here, the media or the government? It seems that you, as a virulent representative of the media, are Big Brother disrobed. Aren't you? Aren't you, Verity?"

Verity's complexion faded to a ghostly apparition, vertigo began overtaking him, then Rooney's voice boasted on his earphone, "Why hello, Verity, it's your old friend Rooney. We're now emailing your profile to everyone in the press so they can spin it and feed it to the blogs, where they'll shit all over you. Your revolting photo will be in morning editions and on cable networks all over the world. Welcome to the truth. Welcome to your judgment day. Be careful what you wish for."

Verity yanked the earpiece out. Tossed it at the audience. He screamed something unintelligible. He saw authorities surrounding the stage. The audience was on its feet, clapping, hollering, moving into the aisles as gleefully as piranha in a feeding frenzy.

Video of Mayor Perkins running from the cameras transitioned on the mighty screen to Wissel laughing, then to Verity's horrifying countenance, then to his judgmental glare. His eyes floating on a black screen that he used to watch, to strike fear into, his followers, appeared on top of the screen. Images faded to words: "Oliver Wissel wants to profile you."

The arena disintegrated to chaos. The Republican senator began taunting, "Verity, Verity . . ." The audience picked up the chant. His name, his online moniker, so much of his truth was public; he grabbed his face and saw his photo there two hundred feet high; he looked down again at his hands, his feet. His name thumped on a quickening pulse through all of himself, smashing his ego, pummeling his blind conception of himself into seeing his own flesh, to seeing himself completely for the first time in decades.

He scratched his face with his nails, dislodging a fake nose, turning his toupee askew, drawing blood.

Cameras focused on him. His live picture took over the screen. There his image was, a color shadow standing two hundred feet tall. A live feed of sweat smearing makeup, of his toupee falling to the stage, of the real person, whatever his name was, bleeding through his magnificent disguise as he looked up at himself falling apart in front of all the world.

Across the screen, under Verity's deteriorating figure, streamed the words: "He wants to profile you, to end privacy. He wants to end your private lives."

A roar ricocheted as the people busted over velvet ropes.

The presidential candidates were whisked away by Secret Service.

A tidal wave of people crashed over the stage and security and smashed into the screen, tossing lecterns over, sending still-live microphones clanging as the massive screen shook and fell upon hundreds of hapless heads.

Verity felt hands pulling off his clothes, smearing his makeup, tearing his suit. People were mauling him. The masses controlled the stage. Officers, FBI, and security desperately tried to keep the people off Verity.

Verity fell to his knees. Special Agent Bent stood over him, swinging his arms, smashing back the tide of humanity. The government wanted Verity. They wanted him in once piece. They wanted his system.

Verity looked up into the faces of the government's secret police and knew what they'd do to him, what they'd get out of him. He kneeled within the chaos. He slouched over as feet slammed into his kidneys. He reached into his lapel pocket. Pulled out a white pill. Looked up through the FBI agents protecting him, encircling him, facing their backs to him to keep the people from tearing him apart until a path could be cleared to bring him out.

Verity peered up, right into a camera positioned well over the stage. He stared into the camera and felt its glass eye raping him, seeing everything in him, judging him by his appearance, his real appearance, not what he was so sure was inside his spent body. He spit out his fake teeth. He wiped off his fake nose. He sucked a deep breath into his old, shriveled chest.

He put the pill in his mouth. He swallowed.

Pandemonium.

26

I AM ME

MINUTES LATER HANDCUFFS chewed my wrists. Two FBI agents held my forearms powerfully enough to leave bruises where each finger tightened. My head was bowed, my eyes were focused on my shoes. I thought them fine shoes, but I wondered what I'd wear in prison. I realized with some surprise I didn't care. I felt freer than ever before, because this was a role I'd chosen freely, with complete knowledge of right and wrong, justice and injustice. I'd made a stand. And it was good.

I could hear thousands stomping, hollering above. The Garden had the sound of a dance club as techno bass pounded and people formed a mosh pit. The stage was still filled with people, all confused, not angry, just excited, exuberant. Exits had been blocked. The FBI was screaming into radios to make Garden security and New York's finest block the doors. They knew all of Verity's followers, his disciples, would be in the building, so they wanted to make the 20,000 in attendance stream out single file so they could get good photos of everyone with the NSA cameras already in position, so they could check all their IDs, construct a database that would later be cross-referenced. But the thing was, more than a few people were afraid of passing through this bottleneck because of crimes they'd committed, many more detested the authoritarian control.

The crowd, many of whom had walked in off the street, wanted none of being corralled down a chute as herders do sheep ready to be sheered. Riot was in the pulse of the audience. The trapped audience wanted out. This was New York, a city of individuals. The government couldn't herd them, not 20,000 of them all penned up in this arena and all addled by what they'd seen, found out.

I looked up, watched the people roiling on the monitors in the production room and thought the unbridled scene seemed symbolic of the overall struggle, of people refusing to be cattle, to be led, branded, slaughtered.

Rooney walked into the production room. He grabbed me by the shoulders, whirled me around and said, "He took something. He swallowed something. It's all in his mouth. He's dead. You knew, you knew, didn't you? You're still one of them."

I shook my head.

"You're gonna fry."

"I have a presidential pardon, Mr. Rooney."

"The hell you have."

"The senator has to save me to save himself, it'll stick."

"Damn you."

"No, damn you," I said as my anger sparked a fire from deep inside. "I saw what you did to Aster."

Rooney grimaced. "How the . . . we had to interrogate."

"Did she even have an attorney present? Did she waive her rights?"

"Fuck you."

"I have video of you questioning her. Don't look at my laptop. I emailed it to new accounts I set up under false names. I've set off an e-bomb that has destroyed all the contents on my laptop and the system used tonight by overwriting them endlessly. You, nor the NSA, can get anything there."

"I knew we shouldn't have let you near those computers."

"I gave you Verity."

"You gave me a dead body."

"I stopped him from setting his system loose, from enabling everyone to destroy privacy. From doing an Old Testament–style flood, in this case of personal information, designed to wipe the world clean of sin by profiling everyone."

Rooney didn't comprehend all that, there was a lot he had to consider. He didn't know what to say, so he stood there bubbling over.

"Aster was also pardoned, Rooney. You'd be smart to let her go right now."

Rooney stepped back, said, "I don't have to do shit until that pardon, if there is one, is in my hands."

I leaned closer, said, "I told you once, you want to work with me, you deal me straight. The hardball stuff doesn't work with me. I'm stubborn, really stubborn. And I'm the only one you know who understands Verity's system. You'd be smart to deal me straight."

"You, why? You're one of them."

"The hell I am."

"Then whose side are you on, you fucking little traitor?"

I leaned even closer and said too calmly for Rooney's liking, "I'm on my side. No one owns me. Not you and definitely not Verity."

"What the hell?"

"I've been a pawn through most of this. You told me to work for Verity, to be a double agent. He wanted the same thing. The lines were blurry until I saw, until I clearly understood what's really going on here, what's really right."

Rooney leaned back away from my judgmental breath, fell against a desk, said, "What are you talking about?"

As a riot began to wreck Madison Square Garden upstairs and all around, security gave up on controlling the exits and instead opened them wide, even yelled for and cajoled the 20,000 to leave, I said, "Big Brother nor Verity are right."

"You want to destroy all we've created?" said Rooney. "To turn back the clock? You're a nut. Go and join the Amish, till the land, and make believe the world is still all agrarian."

"No," I said, "what's right is quite the opposite. Technology can turn back the clock to freedom."

I stepped closer to Rooney and with my hands still cuffed behind my back said, "The NSA, our online police, are doing important things to keep our system safe, but they're also working to keep individual rights weak. They've lost sight of what they're supposed to be protecting, our individual rights."

Rooney was flabbergasted. "You're an idealist."

"And proud of it."

Rooney's eyebrows rose. He didn't know what to say.

"Digest this, Rooney: What Verity did, was trying to do, was by design. He wanted me, a traitor, to turn him in at the opportune time; when he was on stage in front of America. That way you'd arrest him in public and so couldn't secret him away. But the thing he didn't figure was that I might be able to profile him in public. He thought his Truth Seekers would stop that. He was too arrogant to conceive it was possible. Based on his off-base profile of me, he thought I was a wimp, that I couldn't take bold action. But make no mistake, he did want to be caught. That's why he let me get away with so much. It's why he helped me today. I think he was adjusting his plan to the conditions, but he certainly wanted me to be a Judas."

"What are you talking about?"

"I'll explain later. But just know he wanted to be taken by Big Brother. To go on trial. To be publicly crucified. To slay you in court while exposing you, the government, to the people. It'd have been the trial of the century. He'd have turned the press against you. He would have won that way. And then he'd have to die mysteriously, as a persecuted man that no one knew enough about to humanize. It was how he wanted to start his new order. He saw himself as the messiah of a truer way. By profiling him, by humanizing him, I took that from him. I think that's why he killed himself. Dying became his only option. When he saw he was profiled, he realized he'd lose in court, lose in the public eye. So he took his life hoping the government would whisk his body away and seal the files, that bureaucrats and Washington brass would try to hide this thing. A poor plan B, but one nevertheless, because if the government hides his body and what occurred here, it'll fuel the conspiracy theories, it'll help the movement his disciples will soon be fermenting."

As I spoke I began to fully understand that though we might have stopped Verity's program from profiling America, Verity's cult hadn't been stopped. America needed a public debate, a battle waged for individual freedom. This was just the beginning.

Rooney slouched, realized he had a lot to think about before he decided if I was on to something. He looked at the floor, then back at me and said, "Get those cuffs off him. Get Aster in here. Sidney, you're not free. But, well, if I let you go now will you come in for questioning?"

"I'll come in."

27

ME, MYSELF, AND I AGAIN

"WOULD YOU HURRY?" Aster pleaded as she looked in a mirror in my apartment while doing something awful to her complexion.

I pulled on the blue polyester suit I'd worn when playing Michael Waters as I read the morning newspaper.

It Was To Be A Transparent Nation

New York, November 3—Last night's presidential debate disintegrated into mayhem at Madison Square Garden, and we're just beginning to learn why. Network anchorman Oliver Wissel was pronounced dead at the scene. The cause is as yet unknown. An autopsy will be performed today.

Wissel is currently under investigation for running the online cult "the Truth Seekers" that profiled New York Mayor Bill Perkins and dozens of other politicians during this election season. According to information released while he was acting as the moderator of the presidential debate, Wissel's online alias was "Verity." He allegedly intended to publish a program that could have been used to profile anyone and everyone, especially publicly elected officials. He'd allegedly used this program to illegally eavesdrop on the communications of public officials and to obtain private, possibly even classified materials. More details will be published as they become clear.

At press time six people had been arrested in connection with the Truth Seekers online cult, a group allegedly working for Wissel (aka "Verity"). Four additional members are being sought (see related story, "Profiles of Wanted Cult Members"). The cult members' attorney released a statement claiming religious freedom from prosecution. New York District Attorney Kevin Clark said, "This defense seems as shallow as their true movement."

In what seems to be a related case, Sidney McDaniel and Nancy "Aster" Coldworth, who were both wanted in connection with the Verity profiling case, have been pardoned by the president of the United States.

This quick pardon prompted Rep. Christopher Hartt to say at a press conference this morning, "It makes one wonder, did our esteemed president, who was never profiled, get blackmailed by this two-bit hacker, McDaniel."

In an online statement, McDaniel said, "Verity's computer system was completely destroyed." Authorities now say Verity's intention was to profile the entire nation. His goal was a transparent nation. But according to sources in the Federal Bureau of

Investigation (FBI) his software, if indeed there ever was such a profiling database on America, has been destroyed.

Verity's "profile" can be viewed on the FBI's website along with his photos. There is already a website with a 30-second clip of Verity's caricature doing a two-step/striptease to the American national anthem.

If you're more interested in the real thing, Oliver Wissel's body will be an open-casket funeral beginning tomorrow at the Brooklyn Sacred Heart Mortuary. The curious are sure to file through. But save yourself the gruesome sight, as this Mr. Verity, or whatever his real name turns out to be, is said to be a very ugly individual when without his Wissel newscaster costume.

McDaniel, who was last seen at Madison Square Garden, has informed the press he'll make a public appearance today at 10:00 a.m. . . .

"Sidney, would you put that newspaper down already?" Aster said. "We have to perfect our costumes and you haven't even tried on your glasses yet."

As she puckered her lips and painted them with an awful shade of purple lipstick, she critiqued, "Oh, your eyebrows are all crooked. They look like woolly worms loose on your face."

I slapped on my eyebrows and dashed frantically about as if there really were caterpillars crawling over my face.

Aster giggled, then forced her expression back into her serious lawyerly pose as she put much too much sky-blue eye shadow all around her then gray eyes.

I shrugged as I inspected the ugly black square frames I'd wear and watched Aster gain forty pounds as she strapped on a fat suit. I stopped kidding around then, scratched my head and said, "We're going to be a very homely couple."

"That's the point."

"Yeah, I know, bore them with commonness."

"Exactly."

"Verity was right about this much."

"He was right about more than half of it; that's what made him so damn convincing."

I smiled, put my arms around Aster, and pinched inches on her fake stomach. "My, my, no more double-chocolate Häagen-Dazs for you. But you know, Verity did bring us together. And you're right, he taught me a lot about myself, about this society even. I owe him for that. Though I doubt my father would agree."

"I know some good lawyers who will see your father gets a fair trial," said Aster as she pushed me away. "Now, would you please hurry?"

I considered the drab costume I once used to become the forgettable Michael Waters just a few days before.

Aster giggled. "Rooney sure was peeved that Verity's system is dead and defunct. He seemed so disappointed it wasn't some new virus or something they could use."

Seriousness washed over me for a moment. "Yeah, they would have liked to use his system for their own ends. Just imagine the spying they could have accomplished. But you know, the battle is won, but not the war. There's a lot to do. I destroyed that database and so far, none of the uncaught disciples have done much, but I still have to write an antiviral for Verity's insidious cookie, that thing that infected everything, giving him access to all those private communications. And I have to update security patches to block it."

"Leave all that for now, Sidney, come on, we have like two minutes," she said as she grabbed an ankle-length black dress shaped like a potato sack. "If they see our real faces we'll never be anonymous again. We'll be public figures, or even, heaven forbid, celebrities. I certainly don't want to be one of those love-starved types. The only reasons to become famous are to get rich or to satisfy some need for attention. We have enough money and all the attention I want is yours; besides our careers demand privacy."

I flushed with expectation and said, like I was fantasizing, "Partners . . . we'll rock the cyberworld."

"And maybe even keep Big Brother on the ropes," added Aster. "If Orwell only knew."

As she put those awful glasses on me, Aster thought aloud, "If we show them what we look like, then every time we walk down the street we'll run the risk of someone recognizing us. But if you're a nerdy computer geek—though it's a shame to hide those sincere eyes of yours—and I'm a piggish trailer park queen, then they'll collectively yawn with disappointment and go and feed on some politician, actor, or musician who is just crying out to be loved anyway. Going public just isn't our style."

Then as she rushed again to the mirror she warned, "Now we have to hurry."

"Anonymous again. It sounds like a dream," I said as I looked at my repulsive new face and thought no producer would air it twice.

Aster pulled on a wig as she happily sighed, "Yes, anonymous. True individuals. It is, it is a dream."

THE END

ABOUT THE AUTHOR

FRANK MINITER is an author and investigative journalist. He is the author of *The New York Times* bestseller *The Ultimate Man's Survival Guide—Recovering the Lost Art of Manhood*. His other books include *This Will Make a Man Out of You* and *Saving the Bill of Rights*. Miniter is a contributor to *Forbes* and writes for publications from *National Review* to *America's 1ˢᵗ Freedom*.